He stood there with his focus directly on her, trying to figure out what attracted him to the point where he wanted to strip her naked, right there in his kitchen

But not before he got to taste her again, to see if the flavor of her mouth had changed, and to see if she could still work her tongue as she had before.

His eyes slowly shifted lower to her chest, to the top she was wearing. He pulled in a choppy breath. He saw her nipples start to harden, right before his eyes. Hell, if just a look could do that to her, he wondered what would happen if he were to touch her, taste her.

He could feel his own eyes darkening with heat and knew the moment she saw it, as well. She continued to hold his gaze, then asked, "Is there something else?"

He couldn't help the smile that touched his lips, a predatory one at best. She could ask the damnedest questions. This time he would give her an answer and he hoped she was ready for his response. "Yes, there is something else," he said, walking toward her.

Books by Brenda Jackson

Kimani Romance

Solid Soul
Night Heat
**Beyond Temptation*
**Risky Pleasures*
In Bed with Her Boss
**Irresistible Forces*
**Intimate Seduction*
Bachelor Untamed

*Steele Family titles

Kimani Arabesque

Tonight and Forever
A Valentine Kiss
Whispered Promises
Eternally Yours
One Special Moment
Fire and Desire
Something to Celebrate
Secret Love
True Love
Surrender

BRENDA JACKSON

is a die "heart" romantic who married her childhood sweetheart and still proudly wears the "going steady" ring he gave her when she was fifteen. Because she's always believed in the power of love, Brenda's stories always have happy endings. In her real-life love story, Brenda and her husband of thirty-seven years live in Jacksonville, Florida, and have two sons.

A *New York Times* and *USA TODAY* bestselling author of more than sixty romance titles, Brenda is retired from a major insurance company and now divides her time between family, writing and traveling with her husband, Gerald. You may write Brenda at P.O. Box 28267, Jacksonville, Florida 32226, by e-mail at WriterBJackson@aol.com or visit her Web site at www.brendajackson.net.

BRENDA JACKSON

Bachelor Untamed

BACHELORS *in* DEMAND

To the love of my life, Gerald Jackson, Sr.

To all the members of the Brenda Jackson Book Club.
This one is for you.

Apply your heart to instruction,
and your ears to words of knowledge.

—*Proverbs* 23:12

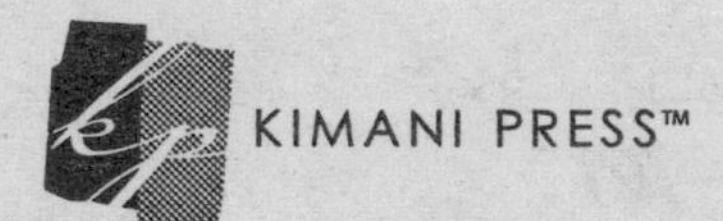

Recycling programs for this product may not exist in your area.

ISBN-13: 978-0-373-86132-3

BACHELOR UNTAMED

www.kimanipress.com

Printed in U.S.A.

Dear Reader,

I love starting a new series!

I can recall when I wrote the first books of my Madaris, Westmoreland and Steele series. It felt wonderful introducing my readers to a family I had created in my mind and held in my heart. I am proud to now introduce to you six men whose ties that bind them forever were created by their fathers, best friends in college.

I envisioned six men, close friends, deciding their lives would be connected forever through their offspring and making their firstborn sons godbrothers to each other. What also would be unique was that their first names would be taken from the last six letters of the alphabet.

I would like to introduce you to Uriel Lassiter, Virgil Harrison, Winston Coltrane, Xavier Kane, York Ellis and Zion Blackstone. Xavier was introduced in my Steele series book four, *Risky Pleasures,* and Uriel was introduced in Steele series book six, *Intimate Seduction.* These six guys, for various reasons, are members of the Bachelors in Demand Club, and are determined to stay single for as long as they can. It will be fun to see how many will retain their membership when the right woman comes along.

Book one, *Bachelor Untamed,* is Uriel Lassiter's story and his leading lady is someone from his past, Ellie Weston. And although Uriel wishes otherwise, she is also someone for his future.

I hope you enjoy reading Uriel and Ellie's story.

Happy reading!

Brenda Jackson

Prologue

"Go ahead and do it, El. You've been dying to kiss him forever. Do it. I dare you."

Ellie Weston rolled her eyes at her best friend Darcelle Owens's statement. She was used to Darcy getting them in trouble with her dares. But, this was one dare that she was more than tempted to carry through.

The two of them stood hiding in the thicket of trees and bushes while spying on the guy Ellie had had a crush on forever. It didn't matter that Uriel Lassiter was twenty-one to her sixteen and a senior in college. All that mattered was how her heart started beating fast in her chest whenever she saw him.

"Come on, El. He's leaving tomorrow to go back home, and you're going to hate yourself for a missed opportunity. This will probably be the last time you'll see him until who knows when. He graduates next spring and will probably never come back here for the summer."

Ellie felt a thump in the pit of her stomach and pondered Darcy's words. With Uriel graduating from college next year, he probably wouldn't be coming back to the lake, at least not as often. Uriel's parents owned a summerhouse right next door to her aunt's home on Cavanaugh Lake, a few miles outside of Gatlinburg. For a entire month during the summer she would visit her aunt, and it was only then when she would see Uriel. The thought that she might not ever see him again was too painful to think about.

She could recall only one summer that he hadn't come, and that had been last year. She'd heard that he and his five godbrothers had taken a trip abroad that summer. It had been the most boring summer of her life.

Ellie glanced over at Darcy and whispered, "If I take you up on your dare, what do I get?"

Now it was Darcy's turn to roll her eyes. "I would think to lock lips with your dreamboat would be enough. But since you want to be greedy, if you take me up on my dare you can have my autographed picture of Maxwell."

Ellie's eyes widened. She had been scheduled to go to that Maxwell concert with Darcy, but had come down with the mumps and missed it. "You'll risk the chance of losing that?" she asked, since she knew what a big Maxwell fan Darcy was. She probably sang "Fortunate" in her sleep.

"Yes, but only if the kiss lasts for more than a minute. I don't want to see just a peck on the lips, El. You're going to have to make him kiss you for a long time."

Ellie was aghast. How was she supposed to do something like that, when she'd never kissed a boy before? "Any bright ideas how to pull that off?"

Of course Miss-Know-It-All Darcy would have all the answers. "You're going to have to use your tongue. I heard Jonas tell one of his friends that he liked kissing girls who used their tongue."

Ellie lifted a brow. Jonas was Darcy's oldest brother, who was a senior in high school, so he would know. All the girls back home in Minneapolis just loved Jonas and he loved all the girls. "And he said guys actually liked it?" Ellie asked, to be sure.

Darcy nodded her head. "Yes, I heard him say it. He and Leroy Green didn't know I was hiding under the bed."

Ellie knew better than to ask Darcy what she was doing hiding under her brother's bed. "Well, okay. But if he doesn't want to keep his mouth on mine I can't make him. But I'll try."

Darcy's eyes brightened. "You're going to do it?"

Ellie released a deep breath. "Yes, but you can't make a sound."

"Okay, but remember the kiss has to last for at least a whole minute."

Ellie frowned. "You don't have to remind me."

Uriel glanced to the side when he heard the sound of footsteps crunching on fallen leaves.

Ellie Weston.

Good grief! She was only sixteen, but last week when he had arrived to join his parents at the lake, he hadn't been able to believe how much she changed since two summers ago. She was no longer a tall, lanky girl, but now she had curves in places that he couldn't help notice.

She had been wearing a pair of shorts and a blouse and she looked quite stunning. The fitted top she wore outlined breasts that were full and perfectly formed. She had the tiniest waist he'd ever seen, and her hips flared out rather nicely, to join a pair of gorgeous long legs.

He swallowed, trying not to notice how she was dressed now. She was wearing another pair of shorts and they were way too skimpy for his comfort. And the way her blouse fit exposed a sliver of her bare stomach.

He frowned, trying to deny the attraction. He was five years older than her, and shouldn't be thinking about her this way. Damn, but he could remember when she was a kid in braces climbing trees. Now he could imagine them hooking up as a couple. He shook his head slightly to clear his thoughts.

"Hey, Uri. What are you doing?" she asked, coming closer.

He shifted his gaze from her legs to glance out over the lake. "Fishing. Where's your friend?" He nearly let his fishing rod fall in the water when she came and sat on the pier beside him.

"Oh, Darcy's taking a nap. We were both up late last night."

He forced his gaze to stay straight ahead. "Why aren't you taking a nap, too?"

"Umm, not sleepy. I was taking a walk, and then I saw you and thought I'd come keep you company."

He was about to tell her not to do him any favors, but decided against it. She had no way of knowing he was seeing her in a whole new light. Her aunt, Ms. Mable, would probably kill him if she knew what kind of light that was.

"So, how is college?" she asked him.

He shrugged. "It's okay. What about you? Are you looking forward to the end of the summer to head back to school?"

She giggled. It wasn't a kid's giggle, either. It had a sensuous twang to it. At least he thought so. "Heck no. I don't like school. I can't wait to get out," she said.

He heard her words and recalled feeling that way when he'd been her age. "Don't you have plans to go to college?" he couldn't help but ask.

"No. I want to get married."

Now that got his attention and he couldn't help but glance over at her. Then he wished he hadn't. She had brought her face close to his. Too close. He could actually see the dark irises staring back at him. That cute little mole on the side of her nose was even more visible. And the shape of her lips… When had they gotten so full? So well defined?

He swallowed, tried forcing his gaze back to the lake, but his eyes refused to budge. "Why do you want to get married?"

She smiled and his gut pulled so tight he could barely breathe. "I want to get married because…"

Her voice had lowered and he could barely hear her words. And was he imagining things, but had she just inched her face a little closer to his? Or was he the one leaning in closer?

"Because of what?" He somehow found his voice to

ask her, and couldn't stop his gaze from dropping from her eyes to her lips.

"Because I want to know how it is to sleep with the man I love. To feel his body beside me in bed. To become acquainted with his lips on mine."

He felt himself leaning in closer to her. "Aren't you too young to be thinking of such things?" he managed to ask in a voice so deep he barely recognized it as his own.

"No." And then in a move that was totally unexpected, she leaned over and plastered her lips to his.

The first thought that came to his mind was to push her away, but her lips felt so soft and sweet that he found himself entranced. His body shuddered as he sank his hand into her hair, deepening the kiss.

"That's it, El. Hang on in there! You've made the one-minute mark, so now you can go for the gusto!"

Uriel jerked up, and in the process nearly tumbled them both into the water. He had to catch his breath before he could say anything, and then he looked from Ellie Weston and her thoroughly kissed lips, to her friend, the one that should have been napping.

He narrowed his gaze, first at the other girl and then at Ellie. "What's going on, El?" he asked in a rough voice.

Before Ellie could reply, Darcy spoke up, grinning proudly, "You kissed her for one minute and twelve seconds, so she won the dare."

Those words hit him hard in the chest. That kiss had been part of a dare. He had been the butt of these girls' joke? That very idea made his blood boil and intense anger rushed through him. He glanced over at Ellie. "Is that true, El?"

Her face had tinted in embarrassment, and she looked everywhere but at him, mostly glaring over at her friend. "I asked you a question, El," he said, when she didn't say anything.

She drew in a deep breath and then glanced back over at him and said. "I can explain, Uri."

He shook his head. "No explanations. Just answer the question. Was that kiss about a dare between you and your friend here?"

"Yes, but—"

Not giving her a chance to say anything else, he snatched up his fishing rod and angrily began walking off the pier. He got halfway, turned back around and said directly to Ellie, "The next time I come to Cavanaugh Lake, I'm going to make sure that you aren't here."

And then he turned around and kept walking, while wishing that he could forget the sweet taste of her lips.

Chapter 1

Ten years later

"To Flame, with all my love. D."

Ellie Weston studied the elegant sprawling handwriting across the bottom of a framed picture on the wall in her aunt's bedroom.

She lifted a brow. Aunt Mable had probably purchased the painting at one of those garage sales she'd enjoyed getting up on Saturday mornings to drive forty miles into Knoxville to attend. In fact, Ellie had noticed several new paintings in all of the bedrooms, as well as the living room. However, this particular one caught Ellie's eye because it wasn't one she would have expected her unmarried seventy-year-old aunt to be attracted to.

Ellie studied the painting some more. It was a colorful piece of art that showed a faceless but very naked couple in a risqué embrace. So much in fact, that upon closer study it appeared they were having sex.

She felt a heated blush stain her face as she stepped back and glanced around. It seemed that rather recently her aunt had gotten a new bedroom suite—a king-size Queen Anne four-poster bed in beautiful cherry mahogany. The bedroom suite had a romantic flair that Ellie liked. And there was a matching desk in one section of the room with, of all things, a computer. When had her aunt entered the computer age? Ellie hadn't been aware she'd owned one. If she'd known, they could have been staying in contact by e-mail.

To Ellie, her aunt's two-story house had always seemed too large for one person. It had a spacious layout that included a huge living room, a bathroom, dining room and eat-in kitchen downstairs, and four bedrooms and three bathrooms upstairs. The wood paneling had been removed and the walls had been painted an oyster white. The bright color actually made the entire interior appear larger, roomier.

Had it been five years since she had last visited her aunt here? Although she had stopped coming to the lake house when she'd turned twenty-one, she and her aunt still got together every year when she could convince Aunt Mable to come visit her in Boston, where she had moved after college. It had worked well for the both of them. It gave her aunt a chance to leave the lake and visit someplace else, and it gave Ellie a chance to not dwell on the most embarrassing memory of all her visits here.

She had stopped speaking to her best friend Darcy for an entire month after that kissing incident with Uriel Lassiter, regardless of the number of times Darcy had told her how sorry she was for getting carried away with her excitement. In the end, Ellie had accepted full responsibility for ever accepting Darcy's dare in the first place.

And it was her fault that Uriel had kept his word and had made sure their paths never crossed at Cavanaugh Lake again.

She had not seen him in ten years. He had been out of the country, unable to attend her aunt's funeral last month, but her parents had mentioned getting a nice floral arrangement from him.

Ellie shook her head, remembering that Uriel's parents had gotten a divorce two years ago. Who would have thought the Lassiters would ever split? And according to her parents, Carolyn Lassiter was now involved with a much younger man, one only a few years older than her own son.

The last Ellie had heard, according to Aunt Mable before she'd died, was that Anthony and Carolyn Lassiter were in court, battling over who would get ownership of the lake house. As a result of the bitter embroilment, the courts had ruled that the house should be put up for sale and the proceeds split. Aunt Mable had no idea who'd bought the lake house next door and hadn't met her new neighbor before she'd died.

Deciding she needed something to eat before she began unpacking, Ellie left her aunt's bedroom and began walking down the stairs, remembering how her aunt, who hadn't been sick a day in her life, had died peacefully in her sleep. Although Ellie knew she would miss her, she felt it was befitting for her to go that way—without any type of sickness to destroy her mind and body. And from what she could tell, although Aunt Mable had probably been lonely at times living out here at the lake, her aunt was happy. At least she had appeared happy and content the last time Ellie had seen her. And she had left everything she owned to her one and only grandniece. Ellie was overwhelmed by such a grand gesture of love.

She walked into the kitchen and immediately noticed the new cabinets. It seemed her aunt had given the house a face-lift, one that had been beautifully done. There were new marble countertops, stainless steel appliances and polished tile floors.

The drive from Boston had been a long one, and Ellie had stopped by one of those fast-food places to grab a hamburger, fries and a shake before getting off Interstate 95. Then, once she had reached Gatlinburg, she stopped at a market to pick up a few things for dinner, deciding that later in the week she would take an inventory of what she would need for her month-long stay at the lake. It was a beautiful day, the first week in August, and the first thing Ellie intended to do tomorrow was open up the windows to air out the place. The living-room window was huge, wall-to-wall, floor-to-ceiling and provided a lot of sunlight and a beautiful view of Cavanaugh Lake, no matter where you stood or sat.

Crossing the kitchen floor, she opened the pantry and wasn't surprised to find it well stocked. Her aunt was known to prepare for the winter months well in advance. Settling on a can of soup for dinner, she proceeded to warm it on the stove.

Standing at the kitchen sink, she glanced through the trees to look at the house that used to be owned by the Lassiters. She could easily recall how often she would stand in this very spot, hoping for a glimpse of Uriel when he would come outside. But she had discovered long ago that the best view from her aunt's bedroom window was that of the backyard and pier.

A half hour later, Ellie had finished her soup and was placing her bowl in the sink when she glanced out the window and saw that a car was parked in front of the house next door. She lifted a brow, wondering if perhaps the new owners had decided to spend some time at their lake place.

Ellie had parked her car in the garage, so they would not know someone was in residence at her place. Her place. That seemed so strange, when this home had belonged to Aunt Mable for so long.

She was about to turn around and go upstairs to start unpacking when something caught her eye. She drew in a tight breath as she leaned closer toward the window to make sure her eyesight wasn't playing tricks on her.

The man who had come to stand outside on the front porch, while talking on a cell phone, was older-looking now, but was just as handsome as she remembered. She was twenty-six now, which meant he was thirty-one.

She might be mistaken, but it appeared he had gotten taller. She figured his height to be at least six foot three. The T-shirt he was wearing covered broad shoulders and his jeans were molded to firm thighs. Her gaze slid to his face. The color of dark chocolate, his features were and always had been striking, a pleasure to look at.

Ellie scanned his face, from the thick brows that canopied a pair of beautiful dark eyes, to the long, angular nose that sat perfectly in the center of his face and more than highlighted the sensuous shape of his lips, to the perfect lines of his jaw. Strong. Tight. Every feature was totally flawless. Him standing there in his bare feet made her think of a chocolate marshmallow all ready to eat.

The thought of that made her stomach stir, generated a tingling sensation even lower, and it made the nipples of her breasts that were pressing against her blouse feel achy. She quickly moved away from the window, crossed the room and sat down at the table.

Uriel Lassiter had returned to the lake house, and the one thing she knew for certain was that he hadn't made sure she wasn't there.

Uriel threw his head back and laughed. He was still in shock. One of his closest friends from college, who was also one of his investment partners, had called to let him know he was getting married. He just couldn't believe it. Who in their right mind would have thought that there was a woman somewhere capable of winning the heart of Donovan Steele. *The* Donovan Steele. The man who always claimed he wanted to be buried wearing a condom, because even then he knew he would be hard.

Uriel had the pleasure of meeting Donovan's woman a few weeks ago. With a PhD and a professorship at

Princeton, Natalie Ford had just as much brains as she had beauty. And she *was* a beauty. That was one of the first things Uriel had noticed that night when she had come storming into the Racetrack Café, ready to give Donovan hell about something. Evidently, their disagreement had gotten resolved, since Donovan was now talking about a wedding.

"Hey, Don, we're going to have to get together when I return to Charlotte," he said. "And we'll make it one hell of a celebration. Have the two of you set a date yet?"

"We're having a June wedding," Donovan replied easily. "After we marry, she'll take a sabbatical to write another book and work on several projects with NASA. You can't imagine how happy my family is."

Uriel could just imagine. Donovan, the youngest of the Steele brothers, headed the Product Administration Division of the Steele Corporation, and Uriel was Vice President of Lassiter Industries, the telecommunications company his father, Anthony Lassiter—CEO and president—had founded over thirty-eight years ago.

Although both he and Donovan had major roles at their family-owned businesses, years ago, right out of college, they had partnered in a co-op. They had started out by flipping real estate, and later moved on to small businesses. The co-op had proven to be highly successful, and they had moved on to even larger investments, like the publishing company they had recently purchased.

Two years ago, Uriel's father had taken a leave of absence due to stress and depression brought on when the wife he'd been happily married to for over thirty-five years asked for a divorce. That had forced Uriel to take over the day-to-day operations of Lassiter Industries.

Uriel was glad his dad had finally snapped out of his depression, decided life was too short to drown in self-pity over a woman whom you still loved but didn't want you, and had returned to Lassiter Industries sharper than ever. Uriel had quickly turned things back over to him and decided to take some much needed R and R. The lake house was his first choice. His parents had been forced to sell it, so he decided to be the buyer.

"While you were in Princeton yesterday, I signed my part of the paperwork, so that the consulting firm could proceed with our most recent acquisition," he said of the publishing company they'd just purchased. "Now, you need to make sure you swing by their office on Friday to put your John Hancock on the papers, so they can officially begin going through the books to see what areas we want to keep and those we want to trim.

"I know Bronson has a race next weekend in Michigan, and I promise you'll be out of Manning's office in no time just in case you're planning to go," he added, mentioning their friend, Bronson Scott, who raced for NASCAR.

"Yes, I'm going and will be taking Natalie with me. I can't wait to introduce her to the world of auto racing. What about you? Will you be there?" Donovan asked.

"Umm, not this time. With Dad back at the helm at Lassiter Industries, I'm staying here at the lake for an entire month, and plan on getting in a lot of fishing. And I did bring some papers with me on the publishing company, to do my own evaluation. I'll let you know what I come up with, and I'll compare it with the recommendations of those consultants."

Less than five minutes later, Uriel was ending the call with Donovan. He slipped his cell phone in the back pocket of his jeans and decided to sit down on the porch swing his father had built for his mom years ago.

His mom.

Uriel could only shake his head with sadness whenever he thought of her and the pain she had caused his father. The pain she had caused him. When his parents had first told him they were getting a divorce, they'd shocked the hell out of him. All it took was to see the hurt and sadness in his father's eyes to know that a divorce hadn't been Anthony Lassiter's idea.

Neither of his parents had wanted to talk about the reason for the divorce, and had asked that he simply accept their decision. It hadn't taken long for him to find the reason. His mother had been going through a midlife crisis, which had been evident when she'd hooked up with a boy-toy within months of leaving his father. His mother, for God's sake, was openly living with a man only six years older than him.

Carolyn Lassiter, he had to admit, was a beautiful woman at fifty. The first time Uriel had seen her lover with her at a restaurant, Uriel had wanted to smash the dude's face in. No man wanted to think of his mother in the arms of any man other than his father.

Her actions had not only nearly destroyed his father, but had left a bad taste in Uriel's mouth where marriage was concerned. That was the reason he had joined the Guarded Heart Club, a private fraternity he and his five godbrothers had established. Each had his own reasons for wanting to remain a bachelor for life.

He was about to get up from the pier and go inside, when he glanced through the trees at the house next door. He'd been sorry to hear about Ms. Mable's passing and missed her already. Whenever his parents would arrive for their three-month summer stay, the older lady would be there ready to greet them with a cold pitcher of the best lemonade he'd ever drunk and a platter of her mouth-watering peanut butter cookies.

He pulled in a deep breath thinking how much he loved it here. Gatlinburg was less than ten miles away, and there were only two houses on Cavanaugh Lake. The only other homes were about five miles down the road on Lake Union. Both lakes were nestled in a wooded area within a stone's throw of the Smoky Mountains.

The fresh August air filled his lungs. Nothing relaxed him more than sitting on the pier with a fishing rod in his hand and a cooler of beer not far away. As he'd mentioned to Donovan, he brought along some reading material, but he would work it in. At the moment, well-deserved R and R was at the top of his agenda.

He stretched his body thinking after taking a nap he would go skinny-dipping. It was something he could truthfully say he'd always wanted to do. Now he had the chance. With the house next door vacant, he didn't have to worry about shocking the socks off anyone.

He lay back and looked forward to his naked swim, all alone in the lake.

Chapter 2

Ellie finished putting the last piece of her clothing away, after deciding to sleep in her aunt's bedroom instead of the guest room she'd used whenever she would come to visit. Tomorrow she would start going through her aunt's things. She would donate the clothes to the Salvation Army, and any items of her aunt's that Ellie considered as keepsakes would be put away in the attic, to one day be passed on to her offspring.

She could only shake her head, wondering how she could think of a family when she didn't even have a boyfriend. Her last serious relationship had been a few years ago, right out of college.

His name was Charles Wilcox, and the affair had lasted far longer than it should have. Never had she met a more boring man, one whose sole purpose in life other than his job as a computer programmer was his fixation with pro wrestling. He practically lived for the *WWE Smackdown.*

She had landed her first job after college as a financial advisor with a major bank, and she thought her career was set for a while—only to get laid off in the first year. Instead of trying to compete in a job market that hadn't seemed to be going anywhere, she decided to go back to college to obtain her masters degree. She had graduated last week, but intended to chill a few months before going back into the job market.

She glanced out the bedroom window. The sun had gone down and pretty soon night would come, and she would need to turn on the lights. Once she did, there was no way Uriel wouldn't know someone was occupying her aunt's home. Would he immediately assume it was her? And if he did, would he hightail it back to Charlotte?

But then, there was a possibility he didn't even remember what had happened that summer day on the pier. After all, ten years had passed. However, she could not forget the ice-cold look he had leveled at her when he'd pretty much told her he never wanted to see her again.

She was about to leave the room to go downstairs when the ringing of her cell phone stopped her. Her parents were presently out of the country, taking a well-earned vacation in the Bahamas. It was probably them checking to see how she was doing. Being the only child, she'd always had a special relationship with her parents.

A quick check of the caller ID screen indicated the phone call was from Darcy and not her parents. "Hello."

"What's up, El? You didn't call to let me know you'd arrived safely."

Ellie smiled. Darcy was acting the mother hen as usual. "Sorry, but I got busy as soon as I got here," she said, dropping into the chair next to the window.

"Have you started going through your aunt's things yet?"

"No, not yet. I've decided to put it off until tomorrow. Right now the only thing I want to do is rest. I don't care if I ever read another book again," she said.

Darcy laughed. "Hey, you just haven't read the right book. Now that you have time, you need to read one by Desiree Matthews."

Ellie rolled her eyes. Darcy, who was a corporate executive with the city of Minneapolis, had gotten married right out of college and had gotten a divorce within the first year, when her husband, Harold, began showing abusive tendencies. The first time it happened, by the time the police arrived, Harold had been on the losing end, discovering how well his wife could defend herself. Evidently, Darcy had never told him she had taken karate while growing up.

"Thanks, but no thanks. I don't need to read a book that gets me all hot and bothered," Ellie said, pushing the curtain aside when she thought she saw movement through the trees.

"Trust me, reading about it is better than doing something stupid like making booty calls. Besides, sex isn't all Desiree Matthews's books are about. They're love stories, and there's plenty of romance between the two people. You root for the hero and heroine to work out their problems and get together."

"Yippee," Ellie said, rolling her eyes and twirling her

finger in the air. “Romance or sex is the last thing I need right now. You have a tendency not to miss what you never got a lot of anyway.”

“Yeah, I guess so. And speaking of romance and sex, did that guy you went out with two weeks ago call you back?”

Ellie shook her head. “Nope. Just as well. He was ready for us to make out on the first date, and that wasn’t going to happen.”

She was about to pull the curtains together when something again caught her gaze. She strained her eyes to look through the trees and blinked, not believing what she was seeing. A naked Uriel Lassiter. “Damn.”

“El? What’s wrong? Why did you curse just now?”

“Trust me. You don’t want to know,” she said, easing back from the window so she couldn’t be seen, but keeping her gaze glued to the man walking toward the pier.

“I do want to know. What is it? Tell me. Tell me now.”

Ellie wanted to roll her eyes at Darcy’s persistence, but didn’t. If she rolled her eyes she might miss something, and she intended to keep her gaze focused on Uriel.

“Ellie Mable Weston, tell me!”

Seeing that Darcy wasn’t about to let up, she said, “It’s Uriel.”

There was a pause. And then, “Uriel Lassiter?”

“Yes.”

“He’s there at the lake house? Oh, El, that’s wonderful.”

“What’s so wonderful about it?” Ellie asked, as she continued to stare at Uriel. The only wonderful thing she could think of at the moment was seeing such a nice looking hunk of dark chocolate. The man was built, superbly so. She wasn't close enough to see his front, but his profile and back were simply magnificent.

Ellie couldn't believe that he was walking around stark naked, regardless of the fact he assumed no one was living at her aunt's place.

"I think it's wonderful that he's ten years older and so are you. Chances are, he's forgotten all about that stunt we pulled that summer."

"Don't count on it. Some men have long memories."

"Well, what did he say to you when he saw you? Did he act like he is still angry?" Darcy asked.

"He doesn't know I'm here yet. I'm upstairs in my aunt's bedroom and watching him through the window."

"Oh. What is he doing? What is he wearing?" Darcy asked excitedly. As usual, she wanted every single detail. "Has he changed much over the years? Is he still good-looking?"

"Nothing."

"Nothing? What do you mean, nothing?"

"Darcy, please keep up. You asked what Uriel was doing and what he was wearing, and the answer to both questions is nothing."

There was a pause. "Nothing? Are you saying the man is naked?"

"Yep, that's what I'm saying. I think he's about to go skinny-dipping in the lake."

"What parts of him can you see?" Darcy was not ashamed to ask.

"Mostly the back—and before you ask, the answer is yes. He is as fine as fine can be. Extremely well built.

It's quite obvious that he works out regularly." Ellie nervously bit her lip when Uriel eased into the water. It was only then that she rested her eyes. "I shouldn't be spying on him like this. It's not right."

"Hell, yes it is," Darcy almost screamed in her ear. "If I was there I would be pulling out a pair of binoculars and getting an eyeful. Men are known to girl-watch, so what's wrong with us boy-watching?"

Ellie smiled at the logic in that. "Nothing. But then I shouldn't be discussing it with you."

"Why not? We tell each other everything. Don't try holding out on me now."

Ellie couldn't help but laugh at that. She glanced back at Uriel. He was just getting out of the water, and when he pulled himself up onto the pier, he was facing her and she nearly caught her breath. The man was an Adonis. Perfect in every way.

As if in a trance, she rose from her seat to lean closer to the window, literally pressing her face against the glass to see more clearly, to check out every inch of him. Her gaze took in his wet, muscular thighs, strong-looking legs, tight abs—and she blinked at what she saw at the apex of his legs. His thick shaft seemed to glisten proudly in the sunlight as it lay nested in a thick, curly bed of hair.

At that particular moment he had to be the most beautifully built man she'd ever seen out of clothes. And her eyes took their fill. She stood there entranced. Mesmerized. Captivated. Every bone in his body seemed possessed of strong density: muscular, solid.

She mentally dismissed the familiar landscape that

encompassed him and the body of water surrounding him. The only thing occupying her mind was his body in all its glorious and masculine splendor. Without a stitch of clothing, he appeared rough, unmanageable.

Untamed.

She felt a tug in the pit of her stomach and wondered how it would be to tame such a male. She doubted such a thing could be done. At least not by her.

"Ellie? Are you still there? What's going on? Why aren't you saying anything? What do you see?"

Ellie swallowed tightly. There was no way she could tell Darcy what she was staring at. Barely breathing through constricted lungs, she merely said, "I'll call you back later." Refusing to listen to any argument from her best friend, she clicked off the phone.

As if the clicking sound had the ability to travel through the frame of the house, through the trees and toward the lake, Uriel glanced up toward her house, and before she could move out of the way, his gaze found hers as she stood staring at him through the window like a deer caught in headlights. He returned her stare.

She felt the flush of embarrassment flicker from the top of her head to the bottom of her feet. Uriel Lassiter had caught her watching him in his very impressive birthday suit.

Chapter 3

Uriel's lips formed in a tight line when he recognized the woman who was standing at the window spying on him.

Ellie Weston.

Oddly, he felt not even an ounce of shame at having been caught naked. How was he to have known she was over at Ms. Mable's house?

He grabbed his towel, deciding he had given her enough of a peep show. Since she was still standing there, he wondered if she had a fetish for naked men. Too bad the show was over.

Wrapping the towel around his waist, he broke eye contact with her and began walking back toward his house like he had all the time in the world, fighting the temptation to glance back at her. She was the last person he wanted to see, and in the past he would have asked his parents about her comings and goings at the lake to make sure their paths never crossed. But he hadn't done so this time. Big mistake.

Uriel kept walking, and when he made it to the back door and went inside, he leaned against the kitchen counter and pulled in a deep breath. At a distance, from what he could see through the window, Ellie Weston had grown from a pretty-looking sixteen-year-old to an attractive twenty-six-year-old woman.

He frowned, thinking, so what? It had been expected. Her mother was a nice-looking lady, so Ellie had probably inherited some pretty good genes.

Moving away from the counter he opened the refrigerator and pulled out a beer. He popped the top and took a huge swig, not caring that he was standing, dripping-wet, in the middle of his kitchen. His mind was filled with too many thoughts of the woman he hadn't seen in ten years.

Woman.

It was safe to think of her as a woman now, and not a kid any longer; although, at sixteen, she hadn't really looked like your average kid, not at the rate her body had been developing. Even now he could recall how she had looked that day she and her friend had pulled one over on him.

He wondered how long had she been standing by the window watching him? How much of him had she seen? He would be the last person to admit to being an exhibitionist, and would never have considered a skinny-dip if he'd known someone was next door—especially if that someone was her.

When he finished off the beer, he sat the empty bottle

on the counter, wondering if he was being unreasonable for still holding a grudge after all this time. She had been sixteen, and teenagers had a tendency to act silly and do stupid things. Hell, at that age he could remember all the trouble he and his five god-brothers used to get into. They would spend at least a week together every year while growing up, and would get into and do all sorts of crazy stuff.

He then thought about Ms. Mable and all the kindness she had bestowed upon him as a kid, and even through his adulthood. Although he hadn't made it to the funeral, he had sent a floral arrangement. But he hadn't spoken to anyone in the family.

The decent thing to do would be to go over there and offer his condolences in person. That was the least he could do. Nothing less. Nothing more. In addition to that, the gentlemanly thing to do would be to apologize for going swimming in the nude.

And with that decision made, he moved up the stairs to get dressed.

Ellie paced her bedroom, feeling the heat of embarrassment enflame her body with every step she took. Why did she have to share her most humiliating moments with Uriel Lassiter? First it had been the kiss, and now this. He had actually caught her spying on him while skinny-dipping. She didn't want to think what he probably thought of her for doing such a thing. This was a great way to renew their acquaintance after ten years.

Realizing that wearing out the floor wasn't getting her anywhere, she decided to sit in a chair—the same one she had sat in earlier, before getting into so much trouble. At least now she had pulled the drapes, so if he decided to go streaking across his back porch he would be doing so without having her as a captive audience.

She wished she could place the blame squarely at his feet without feeling guilty. After all, no one told him to parade around without any clothes on. She was a woman. Of course she was going to look. Come on now, get real.

The only thing real about it was how good he had looked. Even from a distance she had appreciated every inch of him that she saw; every body part, individually and collectively. She sighed deeply. When had she developed an interest in male body parts? Probably after seeing such outstanding workmanship on him earlier today.

Her cell phone rang and she didn't have to wonder who it was. No doubt Darcy was calling to see what was going on after she'd all but hung up on her earlier. But given the choice between checking out a naked man and talking on the phone to Darcy, the naked man would win hands down.

She reached for her cell phone. "Yes?"

"Girl, you were wrong for doing what you did. The only reason I'll forgive you is if you say you hung up because you decided to get naked and go join Uriel for a swim."

Ellie rolled her eyes. "You've been reading way too many of those romance novels, Darcy."

"I haven't been reading enough. That's how it goes when you don't have a love life. It's me, a good book and Bruce when I need him. It's safer that way."

Ellie couldn't help but smile. Bruce was the name

Darcy had given her little toy. Her friend was simply scandalous. "You have no reason not to get out and start dating again."

"I do, too. I'm not ready. And until I am, Bruce will have to do. Now, enough about me, what about you and Uriel?"

Ellie frowned. "You're saying it like we're a couple."

"You could be. You've always had a crush on him, you know. Some things you were able to outgrow, but I don't think Uriel Lassiter was one of them."

"I did outgrow him."

"I don't think you did, but I won't argue with you about it. Just tell me how he looks now, and I'll settle for above the waist, since you're determined not to tell be about anything down south."

Settling comfortably in the chair, Ellie closed her eyes and envisioned the much older Uriel. "Oh, Darcy," she said, not realizing how much in awe she sounded. "He was always handsome. But now that I'm older, I see more things than just his eyes that used to make me drool. He has a cute nose and a nice set of lips." Lips she once kissed. "I never realized until today how perfectly they're shaped."

"And you saw all of that from your aunt's bedroom window?"

"Pretty much—especially when he looked up and saw me."

"What! Are you saying he caught you watching him?"

Ellie opened her eyes, feeling her cheeks heat up all over again. "Yes, he caught me, so I can only imagine what he's thinking about now. I acted no better today than I did that day ten years ago."

"He was probably flattered that you were watching.

Men like women who show an interest in their bodies. Besides, like I said earlier, he probably doesn't even remember what happened then. Men typically don't hold grudges."

Ellie wasn't all that convinced. "I hurt his pride. I could see it that day in his eyes. Men don't typically forget something like that. I should have apologized about it. I never did."

"What you should do is let it go and hope he has, too."

Darcy's last words were still ringing in Ellie's ears a full hour later, after she had left the comfort of her bedroom to come downstairs. She planned to go to bed early, to get a good night sleep so she could be well rested in the morning.

Her mom had offered to postpone her vacation to come and help her pack up Aunt Mable's things, but it was something she wanted to do by herself, no matter how long it took. There were a lot of fond memories in this house, and there was no rush. She had an entire month, and if she needed more time she would take it. Her aunt's attorney, Daniel Altman, would be dropping by on Thursday evening to give her a listing of all the bank accounts her aunt had transferred to her name. When she had spoken with him on the phone last week, he'd given her the impression there were several of them.

She found that odd, since her aunt's only source of income that she knew about was the monthly pension check from working forty years as an English professor at the Smoky Mountains Community College.

It had just started to turn dark, and Ellie went through the house, turning on the lights. With the approach of night, she suddenly realized that she had never been here in this house alone. All the times she'd visited, her aunt had been present. She hadn't realized just how quiet things were at night.

Ellie had checked all the doors and was about to go upstairs and settle in for the night, when she heard a knock at the front door. The hard rap against the wood startled her, and automatically her hand flew across her chest at the same time she took a deep breath. The only person she could imagine at her door was Uriel.

The thought of coming face-to-face with him again after all this time gave her pause. Was he coming to have words with her for staring at him through the window? A part of her doubted it, reasoning that if that was the case, he would have done so sooner.

She moved toward the door, inhaling and exhaling deeply. She hadn't expected company, but she figured she looked decent. She had changed her outfit earlier, putting on another shorts set, and a pair of flats were on her feet.

She took a look through the peephole to make certain it was him, but even after verifying that fact, she asked anyway. "Who is it?"

"Uriel Lassiter."

Glancing down again, reassuring herself that she looked okay, and trying to keep her fingers from trembling, she slipped the chain off the door and slowly opened it. Uriel stood there, and at that moment she had to literally catch her breath.

On her porch, while leaning against a post with his

ankles crossed and hands in his pockets, standing beneath the beam of light from a fixture in the ceiling, he looked like he ought to be on the cover of one of those hot and steamy romance novels Darcy enjoyed reading. He had the right height and the perfect build, she thought, trying to keep her gaze from roaming all over him. She had done that enough earlier, and definitely knew how the body beneath the pair of jeans and white shirt looked. And speaking of shirt, she tried not to notice how his was open at the collar, with the first two buttons undone, giving her a glimpse of the spray of hairs there. Something about them nearly had her mesmerized.

She forced her gaze to his face and met his eyes. "Uri, this is a surprise."

Surprise in what way? To see him in clothes instead of naked?

She suddenly realized just how lame her words had sounded, especially after having spent the last few moments checking him out.

"I hope I'm not bothering you this late," he said, in what she thought was a deep and throaty voice. "But once I realized you were here, I felt I should come over and apologize. Had I known, I would have dressed more appropriately for swimming."

Thinking it was probably rude to have him standing on the porch while they engaged in any kind of conversation, she took a step back and automatically he entered inside. "No apology necessary."

And to move on past that, she said, "And how have you been? It's been a while."

A smile touched both corners of his lips and she almost melted into a puddle on the floor. He'd always had a knock-your-socks-off smile. It was still devastating, when he flashed pearly white teeth against chocolate skin.

"Yes, it has been, and I've been fine. What about you? I regret hearing about Ms. Mable. I'm sure her passing was hard on everyone, especially for you. I know how close the two of you were."

"Thanks, and yes, it was, but at least she hadn't been sick or anything. She passed away in her sleep."

He nodded. "That's what I heard."

She recalled that she had more manners than she were presently displaying, and asked, "Would you like to sit down for a minute?"

Belatedly, she realized how that sounded. It was as if she was putting a time limit on how long he could stay. But if he had picked up on it, he didn't show it. He merely crossed the room and sat down on the sofa.

"Would you like anything to drink?" she asked, and then couldn't help noticing how his jeans stretched tight across his thighs when he sat down.

"Yes, thanks. Water will be fine, unless you have something stronger."

She couldn't help but smile, since she'd brought a bottle of wine at a market in Gatlinburg. "Umm, I think I might be able to find something a little stronger. What about a glass of wine?"

"That will definitely work."

"Okay," she said, backing up slowly. "I'll be right back." She then turned, to head straight for the kitchen.

"Take your time."

She glanced over her shoulder and met Uriel's gaze. It was the same gaze that had looked at her earlier, when she'd been standing at the window. She drew in a deep breath, turned back and kept walking.

Her heart was racing a million beats a minute, and she was suddenly beginning to feel a tingle in her inner muscles. Ten years had passed and their parting hadn't been great. Now they were alone. And other than giving him a glass of wine, she had no idea what to do with him.

Uriel pulled in a deep breath the moment Ellie left the room. "Damn," he muttered, and the word nearly got caught in his throat. When he'd seen her standing at the window he knew she had turned out to be a beauty; however, he hadn't figured on that beauty being so spell-binding that it had the ability to strip a man of his senses.

And one of the first things he noticed right off the bat was that she still had the ability to wear a pair of shorts. She still had the flat tummy, curvy thighs and long, gorgeous legs for them. The T-shirt she was wearing was a bit too large for her medium-built frame, but it looked sexy on her instead of baggy.

He tried getting his thoughts together by studying the room. The last time he had been here was about two years ago, right after he'd been told about his parents' divorce. He had needed to get away, and his father had suggested that he come here for the weekend. Ms. Mable had invited him to dinner. It seemed that she had spruced up the place since then. New furniture, new paintings on the wall and a different throw rug on the floor.

"Here you are."

He glanced around and his gaze met Ellie. Another thing he noticed was that her brown hair was shorter. He really liked the stylish cut and thought it was perfect for her oval face. Her almond-shaped eyes were framed by perfectly arched brows, and her high cheekbones blended in well with the sexiest pair of lips he'd ever seen. They had eased into a smile when he mentioned he'd like something stronger than water. That smile had emphasized the smoothness of her mocha-colored skin.

He crossed the room to take the glass from her hand, and suddenly wished he hadn't. The moment their hands touched he felt it: a spark of sensation that went straight to his toes. A quick glance at her face and the surprise she was trying to hide indicated she had felt it as well. "Thanks." He said the words as calmly as he could.

"You're welcome" was her quick response.

He moved to sit back down on the sofa, took a sip of his wine, and after a moment of trying to get his pulse under control, he said, "Your aunt Mable was a special woman. Everybody liked her." He figured discussing her aunt was a safe topic.

"Yes, and I miss her already," she said.

He saw the sad look in her eyes and quickly thought discussing her aunt wasn't a safe topic after all. He took another sip of his wine.

"I understand you've moved back to Charlotte," Ellie said.

He glanced over at her, wondering how she'd known that, and figured her aunt must have mentioned it to her at some point. "Yes, I had moved to Detroit after graduating from college, to open a new branch office of Lassiter Industries, but two years ago I moved back home."

There was no need to tell her that his father had needed him back in Charlotte. The blow of a divorce had ended up being more than Anthony Lassiter could handle.

Evidently his parents' marriage had had issues that even he hadn't known about, hadn't even realized, until they'd announced they were going their separate ways. Even at his age it had been hard on him. It had been even harder to remain neutral and not take sides. He loved them both.

Uriel suddenly picked up on Ellie's nervousness and knew there was something she wanted to ask, even if only out of politeness. So, to make things easier for her, he said, "If you're wondering how my parents are doing since the divorce, they're fine. Dad still goes through life day-to-day, trying to cope, and Mom is out there having the time of her life. She has turned into a real party animal."

He stared down into this wine glass, truly regretting that he might have sounded bitter, but the truth of the matter was that he was. That was something he knew he had to work on.

"And how are your godbrothers?"

He glanced up, as her question made him smile. She had deliberately changed the subject and he appreciated that. She had met all five of his godbrothers during their visits to the lake on several occasions. So she had gotten to know them pretty well.

"They're all doing fine. All successful in their own right."

"That's good to hear. I liked them. They were nice guys."

Uriel chuckled as he took another sip of his wine. She was right, they were nice guys. Most people were only blessed with one good friend, but he had five, which hadn't happened by accident.

Almost forty years ago, his father and five close friends who were in their senior year at Morehouse had made a pledge that not only would they stay in touch after graduation from college, but that they would become godfathers to each other's children, and that the name of each of their first sons would begin with the letters U to Z. The men had kept their promise, and all six sons, Uriel, Virgil, Winston, Xavier, York and Zion, became god-brothers to each other.

"Do you see them often?" she asked.

He met her gaze, deciding it wouldn't be wise to tell her about the club they had formed, the Guarded Hearts Club, and that they met at least once or twice a year, usually on the ski slopes or abroad in Rome, where Zion, who'd become a world-renowned jewelry designer, had lived for the past three years.

"Yes, we get together on occasion, several times a year. They are still single and prefer remaining that way. Don't be surprised if they show up while I'm here."

He then tilted his head, met her gaze and decided it was time they got something out in the open, discuss it if she felt the need, but definitely put it to rest. "And what about that girlfriend you used to hang around? Darcy what's-her-name? Do the two of you still keep in contact?" he asked.

He watched as she shifted nervously in her seat while

taking several sips of her wine. Saying Darcy's name had brought up the past, specifically that day ten years ago, and they both knew it. After taking yet another sip of her wine she met his gaze and said, "Yes, Darcy and I are still close friends. In fact, I talked to her earlier today on the phone. She's divorced and still living in Minneapolis, and she works for the city government there."

She breathed in deeply and then said, "Uriel, about that day when we..."

"Kissed?" He went ahead and supplied the word when he saw she was having trouble doing so.

"Yes. My first kiss, actually. I wanted to see how it was done and decided I wanted you to be the one to show me. Darcy knew it as well, and dared me to take matters into my own hands."

After pausing briefly, she then said, "I owe you an apology. What I did was stupid. But then, during those days I did a lot of stupid stuff."

"I understand," he said, finally accepting that he did. She was right. When you're young you sometimes do foolish things.

"Do you really, Uri?"

He saw the intense look in her eyes. Her need for him to know that she had regretted her actions that day was there for him to see. Evidently, the rift between them had bothered her over the years. Some young women would not have given a damn. But she did.

"Yes, I do," he finally said. "I'd admit at the time I had gotten pretty pissed off about it, but it didn't take me long to get over it."

Now that was a lie if ever he'd heard one. He hadn't

been able to get over it as quick as he'd made it sound, mainly because it had taken him a long time to eradicate her taste from his mouth no matter how many women he'd kissed after that day.

"I'm glad. I'd hoped that you had, but hadn't been sure when I never saw you at the lake again. I knew you came whenever I wasn't here, because my aunt would mention it, and I always assumed it was deliberate."

"Just a coincidence," he said, lying again. No need to send her on a guilt trip. Ten years was ten years. Now they were older, wiser, and from the sexual chemistry he felt flowing in the room, just as attracted to each other. But then, that was the crux of his problem. He never really knew if she'd been attracted to him back then as much as he'd been to her, or if it had been nothing more than playacting as part of her dare with Darcy.

That was a mystery he needed to solve, a curiosity that he needed to explore. "So, how long are you staying out here on the lake?" he heard himself asking her.

"A month."

He nodded. So was he. That meant he had a month to satisfy his curiosity about a few things.

He gave the room one final glance, thinking for some reason that, with all the changes, it now suited Ellie more than Ms. Mable. Everything seemed much too modern for an older woman's taste. It was as if Ms. Mable had somehow known her niece would take up residency here one day.

Uriel returned his gaze to Ellie before placing his wineglass on the table and standing. "I just wanted to come over and apologize about my state of undress earlier today, as well as to convey my condolences regarding Ms. Mable."

"Thanks."

"It's good seeing you again, Ellie. I'll be here for a month, as well, so if you need anything I'll be next door. You can call on me anytime," he offered.

She smiled. "Thanks, Uri, I'll remember that," she said, walking him to the door.

"Do you have a lot of plans for this week?" he asked as they crossed the room.

She shrugged. "Not really. I'll be busy going through Aunt Mable's things. I plan on starting that tomorrow."

"Okay." He paused for a moment and then said, "I'll be going into Gatlinburg on Tuesday to get a bunch of supplies. If you make a list of the things you need I can pick them up as well."

He could tell by the smile on her face that she appreciated his generous offer. "Thanks."

"You're welcome. Good night." And deciding he had stayed longer than he should have, a lot longer than he'd planned, Uriel opened the door and left.

Chapter 4

The next morning, Ellie's eyes opened and she blinked a few times before remembering where she was. Then she closed her eyes, deciding to just lie there for a moment in the big bed until her mind and body became functional. Too much wine last night was definitely to blame for her feeling hungover this morning, a state she didn't need to be in, considering all she had to do today. But she couldn't get herself to move just yet. She wanted to lay there awhile, get herself together while remembering the unexpected visit she'd gotten last night from Uriel Lassiter.

She hugged the pillow to her chest as she remembered how sexy he'd looked sitting on the sofa. It had been nice of him to pay her a visit, to clear the air between them, so to speak. And now, with what happened ten years ago behind them, they could move on and be friends. From what he'd said last night, he would be staying at his lake house for as long as she intended to stay here, which meant they would probably be seeing each other on occasion. She could deal with that. He'd mentioned that his godbrothers would probably be visiting him while he was here. What about a girlfriend?

If she had a man who looked anything like Uriel, she wouldn't let him go anywhere without her for thirty days. Although she'd never heard of him ever bringing a woman to the lake with him before—at least Aunt Mable never mentioned it—Ellie refused to believe Uriel didn't have a special woman in his life. For some reason, she just couldn't imagine him being unattached.

One thing was for certain—although they had both downplayed it last night—sexual chemistry had stirred in the air between them, especially after their hands touched. She had felt a sense of relief when he hadn't acted on it. Some men would have, and she doubted she was ready for the likes of Uriel Lassiter if he were to come on to her. The man was sexual magnetism on legs.

After he left, she had tried doing a few things—had even made an attempt to rearrange her aunt's pantry, which was a wasted effort, since her aunt was known to be meticulously neat. For some reason, she hadn't been able to sleep. After tossing and turning for what seemed like hours, she ended up getting out of bed around three in the morning and indulging in another glass of wine. She didn't remember much after that.

Ellie slowly reopened her eyes and glanced at the clock.

The day had already started without her, and she needed to get out of bed and begin getting some work done.

She had just thrown the quilt off her body, ready to ease out of bed, when a noise outside caught her attention. Deciding she didn't want to be caught staring out the window just in case Uriel had decided to go skinny-dipping again, she slid off the bed and slowly pulled back the curtain and looked out.

She had a clear view of Uriel's backyard, and he was out there jumping rope. And it looked like he was going at it one hundred times a minute. He was shirtless, and the only thing that covered his bottom was a pair of dark-colored gym shorts. No wonder the man was in good shape, with solid muscles. Her gaze scanned his body and she saw he had worked up a sweat. At that moment, her imagination went wild with thoughts of that hot, sweaty body rubbing against hers.

She swallowed deeply as she tried convincing herself there was no need for her to feel guilty about the tingling sensation she was feeling between her legs. After all, she was a woman who hadn't been involved with a man in a while—almost four years now. She had been too wrapped up in schoolwork to care. But with school behind her, her hormones were letting her know she had more time on her hands; and after seeing a naked Uriel yesterday, her body was forcing her to realize that those needs she had placed on the back burner were now clamoring for attention of the primitive kind.

When Uriel stopped jumping rope and leaned over to pick up a set of barbells, she quickly dropped the curtain in place. It wouldn't do well to be caught spying on him again. Besides, she needed to take a shower, get dressed and get some work done.

She made her way to the bathroom, thinking the best thing to do today was to stay busy. Then she wouldn't have a reason to think about her neighbor next door.

Uriel opened his refrigerator and pulled out a bottle of cold water. He chugged it, not caring that a few drops missed his mouth and oozed down his chin to join the sweat on his chest.

He emptied the bottle and wiped his mouth with the back of his hand. He'd needed that. He had doubled the amount of exercises he normally did each morning, just to work off a hard-on that wouldn't go away.

He had awakened around three in the morning, unable to sleep, and had gone outside on the porch to sit a spell. He had known the exact moment the light had gone on in the upstairs bedroom next door, and his gaze had sought out the same window that Ellie had been staring at him from yesterday.

While he sat there in the swing, he had seen her pass by the window a few times before she finally came and stood there with a glass of wine in her hand and a skimpy nightie covering her body. She stared out the window at the lake and sipped her wine. The angle at which the lamp had shone on her had given him a pretty good view of her body through the thin material of her short, bright yellow gown. He had gotten a very private viewing, one he doubted very seriously she knew she was giving. She probably figured that, since his house looked totally dark, he was in bed, asleep. But he hadn't been. His focus had stayed intently on her. He hadn't moved, had barely breathed the entire time.

He was no longer ashamed of the thoughts that had flowed through his mind, or the fact that his senses, as well as his libido, had gotten aroused. She had captivated him enough to sit there in the dark, fighting off occasional mosquito bites, while keeping his gaze glued to her.

From his porch, he hadn't seen all of her, but he had seen enough, and his body had been aching ever since. The thin material of her nightgown had barely covered a curvaceous body and a pair of firm breasts. Because of the way the window was made, he hadn't been able to see anything below her waist, so he could only imagine. And that imagination had gotten the best of him. It still was.

He drew in a deep breath and decided it was time for a cold shower. Since coming of age he'd had his share of women, but he'd never been in what he would consider a serious relationship with any of them, and he'd always made absolutely sure the two of them were on the same page. He hadn't wanted any woman to assume anything, and felt it was up to him to make sure they didn't. One or two had tried and were dropped like a hot potato as a result.

Uriel wanted to think of himself as a unselfish lover, and he would be quick to admit to being in control of all his relationships. There hadn't been any woman who'd made him regret walking away. There might be some things beyond his control, but managing a woman wasn't one of them.

As he headed up the stairs for his shower, he decided that he would stay inside most of the day and get some reading done—and try like hell to forget about his next door neighbor. He figured she would be staying inside most of the day, as well.

She'd indicated last night that she would be going through her aunt's things. He wondered if she was up, or if she was still sleeping off the effects of the wine she had downed. He had watched her consume a whole glass at the window, not to mention the glass she'd had while he had been there.

He recalled how he had felt sitting across from her in that living room last night. Once they had cleared the air about what had happened that day ten years ago, he had relaxed and opened up his mind and thoughts to numerous possibilities. Some had been too shocking to dwell on in her presence, so he had left before he was tempted to get into trouble.

He might have retreated last night, and would lay low most of the week, but when he felt the time was right, he would do something that was beginning to vex him. He had kissed the sixteen-year-old Ellie ten years ago, and now he had a strong urge to see how the grown-up Ellie tasted.

Ellie glanced around her aunt's desk. The drawers were locked, and she figured there had to be a key somewhere. A serious expression appeared on her face as she tried to consider just how her aunt's mind worked. Where would Aunt Mable hide the key?

She smiled and then reached out and picked up the framed photo of her and her aunt taken last year when Aunt Mable had visited her in Boston. On this particular night they had gone to a musical featuring a renowned pianist. It had been around Easter and the weather in Boston had been freezing. They were all bundled up in hooded coats while smiling for the camera.

That had been less than six months ago. Ellie fought the tears that threatened to fall at the memory. No, she wouldn't cry. Her aunt had lived a good life, a full life, and she had been happy. Ellie wished she could live as full a life as her aunt had.

Instinctively, she carefully pulled the back off the frame and her smile widened when the key dropped out. Feeling quite smug at her accomplishment, she picked up the key and began opening the drawers. Most of the items, all neatly arranged, were office supplies—computer paper, ink cartridges for the printer, pencils and pens.

She opened another drawer and pulled out a stack of papers that were rubber-banded together. She lifted a curious brow when the first sheet said, in a bold font, *Make me Yours*, by Flame Elbam.

Flame.

Ellie quickly recalled where she'd seen the name "Flame" before and glanced across the room at the risqué painting on the wall. Raising her brow, she settled back in the chair, flipped through the pages and swiftly came to the conclusion that these pages were part of a manuscript. Who did it belong to?

She stopped flipping the pages when a word—one that denoted a male body part—jumped out at her, quickly grabbing her attention. She blinked a few times and then, for clarity's sake, decided she needed to read the entire sentence, but she ended up reading the complete paragraph. Afterward, she swallowed deeply, felt the heat that infused her body and wondered where the heck an ice-cold glass of water was when you needed it. Whew! What on earth was her aunt doing with something like this?

Although that one raw word still stuck out in her mind, Ellie decided she needed to start reading at the beginning and not jump to any conclusions. After all, just because this was found in Aunt Mable's desk really didn't mean anything. Her aunt was a retired English professor, so she was probably editing the book for a former student as a favor.

Ellie figured that had to be it, and she was certain her aunt hadn't started reading the manuscript yet—and could imagine her aunt's gray hair turning a quick shade of white if she had read that passage she'd just read.

Taking the banded papers in her hand, Ellie went to sit at her favorite chair by the window. After she'd settled in comfortably, she began reading.

Uriel reached over to pick up his cell phone. "Yes."

"How are things going, son?"

Uriel smiled, glad to hear his father's voice. "Things are going great, Dad. I've been getting some reading done about that publishing company Donovan and I recently acquired. What about you? How are you doing?" Although his father had returned to work, Uriel was still somewhat concerned about him overdoing things. Long workdays were becoming a norm for Anthony Lassiter.

"I'm doing fine. In fact, I just wanted you to know that I'll be flying out later today for Rome. I have a meeting with one of our distributors there and plan to stay for a few days."

Uriel raised a brow. "Anything serious?"

"No. In fact, it's something one of the managers can handle, but I decided to go myself. Besides, it will give me a chance to see Zion. It's been awhile since I've spent some time with godson number five."

All that was well and good, but unfortunately, Uriel was reading between the lines. His father's eagerness to leave town could only mean one thing. His parents had been invited to the same social function, and instead of making an appearance while his ex-wife paraded her boy-toy around, he had opted to be somewhere else instead—somewhere like another country.

Uriel pulled in a deep breath. "I understand, Dad," he said, and in all honesty he really did. "Have a safe trip."

"I will. And by the way, I ran into Chester Weston the other day, right before he and Nancy left for a vacation in the islands. He mentioned that Ellie would be packing up Mable's belongings at the lake house. Have you seen her yet?"

His father's question triggered memories of Ellie standing at the window last night. "Yes, I've seen her," he said, deciding not to mention to what degree he'd seen her.

And because he didn't want his dad to ask any more questions, he said, "Okay, Dad, I better get back to reading those documents. But if you need me to return to Charlotte to handle things while you're away, then—"

"No, no. The company will be in capable hands while I'm gone. I just wanted to let you know. Take care, Uri."

"You do the same, Dad."

When Uriel hung up the phone a part of him could actually feel his father's pain. He knew that more than ever he needed to have a long talk with his mother. What could she be thinking? He already knew the answer. Only of herself.

Stretching his body, he decided to walk out to the pier for a while. He had been holed up inside reading for a couple of hours now. Walking through the kitchen, he opened the door and stepped out on the porch. Instinctively, his gaze moved to the window across the way.

Uriel squinted his eyes against the sun, and he could see Ellie sitting in a chair by the window, where it seemed as if she was doing the same thing he'd been doing before receiving his father's call. Reading.

He hoped that whatever papers she was reading were a hell of a lot more interesting than the ones he'd just gone over.

Chapter 5

Ellie pulled in a deep breath at the next chapter break, inwardly acknowledging that she evidently had lived a sheltered life. How on earth had the author come up with this stuff? And did people actually do those kinds of things in the bedroom?

Well, to be honest, about eighty percent of the time they weren't in the bedroom, but were in places she would not have thought of making love, not even in her wildest dreams. It was plain to see that the imagination of the person who had written this story was a lot more vivid than hers.

The story wasn't just a bunch of pages filled with nothing but hot and heavy sex. The couple was in love with each other; however, neither were ready to face up to that fact. The reader knew their true feelings, though.

So, all the time the hero claimed that he could never love any woman—that it was nothing more than sex—the reader knew differently. Ellie already knew that the heroine was chipping away at the hard casing that surrounded the hero's heart.

The intimacy they shared in the bedroom was what sexual fantasies were about, and only someone who not only understood the lovemaking act, but who was familiar with it as well, could do these scenes justice. They were gripping, so earth-shakingly passionate. Ellie was dying to find out which of her aunt's acquaintances had that much bedroom experience and passion to pen such a romantic masterpiece.

Ellie thought about the many times Darcy had tried getting her to read a romance novel, and how she had rebuffed the very thought of doing so. Now she knew what she'd been missing.

The only downside to reading about such passion was that it made you realize how much you lacked in your own life. To have a man kiss you to the point that you actually felt like swooning, or to think that something like multiple orgasms could actually occur during a lovemaking session, was too much to consider. But there had been something about the intensity of the love the couple shared that easily took your breath away.

At that moment, her stomach growled and she glanced over at the clock, unable to believe she had read through lunch. She was eager to finish the book, but she knew she had to eat and do a little of what she'd intended to do today. But a part of her couldn't wait to see what the next scene would bring.

Placing the pages on the bed, she stood and stretched. Glancing out the window, she saw Uriel sitting down on the pier, fishing. It reminded her of the day she had pulled that prank on him. Not wanting to remember, she moved away from the window and headed downstairs to the kitchen.

Uriel grimaced. He had been sitting here for a couple of hours and had yet to catch a single fish. For some reason, they weren't biting today, which for him was a huge disappointment as well as an aggravation.

He had stopped reading, to give his eyes a rest. From all accounts, Vandellas Publishing Company, whose home office was in Houston, with a little more than a hundred employees, was financially sound, which was the reason he and Donovan had purchased it. They would hold on to it a few years before reselling it for a profit. That meant they needed to do anything they could to keep it financially sound until then.

He glanced at his watch. One thing for certain was that he wouldn't be enjoying fried fish for supper. He was glad he'd taken a hamburger patty out of the freezer.

Because he couldn't resist the temptation any longer, he glanced over his shoulder to Ellie's bedroom window and noticed she was no longer sitting there reading. He wondered what had captivated her to the point that she'd sat in that chair by the window for at least four solid hours. He wondered too what happened to her plans to go through her aunt's things today.

Reaching the conclusion that it wasn't really any of his business, he turned his attention back to the lake and to another question he was wondering about. Did Ellie have a boyfriend? Was that the reason she'd been standing at the window last night? Had she been hot and restless for a lover who hadn't been able to make the trip with her? Did that mean she would be expecting company any day now?

And why in the hell did the thought of that nag him?

He stared intently at the lake, refusing to dwell on the thought. Hell, if truth be told, he was probably the hot and restless one. He treated sex as the sport it was, and knew, without thinking too hard about it, just when was the last time he'd played. Valentine's Day. The woman was someone he'd met at the Racetrack Café. They had dated a few times before she'd begun getting possessive. She'd found out rather quickly that he didn't do *possessive* very well. On occasion she would call. He had yet to call her back. One day she would learn that most men appreciated women who knew how to curtsy out of the picture gracefully.

He decided he'd spent enough time out here on the pier. He always enjoyed fishing, whether he'd had a good day or not. There was something about sitting on the water, especially Cavanaugh Lake with a fishing rod and a six-pack. It was peaceful and relaxing. That was the main reason he'd bought the lake house from his parents.

He eased into a stand and gathered his tackle box and fishing gear and began walking back toward his house. He glanced up at Ellie's window. She was back, and he immediately felt a tug in his gut. From the looks of things, she was back to reading again.

Something, he wasn't sure what, made her look up at that moment, as their gazes connected. He felt it. More than a mere tug in his gut or a stirring in his blood. It was a rush of desire that he knew had everything to do with how he'd seen her last night while standing at that window. Sexy couldn't get any better.

Figuring they didn't need to pass the time away just staring at each other, he threw up his hand to acknowledge her presence. Smiling amiably, she waved back.

That was that. At least he quickly told himself so. Shifting his gaze away, he kept on walking.

Ellie watched until Uriel was no longer in sight, and thought that he was just as handsome as Grant Hatteras, the hero in the manuscript she was reading. Grant, the man who had captured Tamara Carrington's heart.

In her mind, Uriel had all of Grant's physical attributes. He was handsome as sin and had a body that could make a woman drool. And he could kiss you in a way that made your toes curl. She'd been only sixteen when she'd kissed Uriel, but that single kiss had made a gigantic impact on her and had been the basis of comparison for all the other kisses she'd shared since. No one had come close.

When she'd confided in Darcy about it, her best friend had rolled her eyes and said that every girl remembered her first kiss and thought it was special. But Ellie truly believed that, for some reason, it was more than that for her. And she wanted to believe that Uriel had gotten caught up in the kiss as much as she had, before Darcy had made a mess of things. She couldn't help but wonder how far things would have gone if Darcy hadn't shown up. What if the two of them had been completely alone, with no one spying on them? Would he have been her first in more ways than one?

She drew in a deep breath, thinking that reading about Grant and Tamara was putting her into a romantic mood. She could actually feel the chemistry flowing between them, the surge of energy that would flow from Grant whenever he knew that Tamara was near. Even when they would stand across the room from each other and their gazes would meet, there was something there, a desire that went so deep that merely reading the passages left Ellie breathless.

She glanced around her bedroom, specifically at the clothes hanging in the closet. Aunt Mable's clothes. She was supposed to start packing them up today, but since she had started reading this manuscript, she'd been so entranced she couldn't think of doing anything other than finishing it. So she would. For however long it took. She hadn't taken the time to read for pleasure in years, and if she wanted to take a few lazy days, then she deserved to do so.

With that decision made, she curled up in the chair and continued reading.

Chapter 6

The next morning, Uriel stepped out on the back porch with a cup of coffee in his hand, and glanced around. It would be another beautiful day, and he couldn't help wondering if the fishing would be better today than it had been yesterday. In a few hours, he would grab his fishing rod and a cooler for his six-pack and find out.

He pulled his cell phone out of his pocket when it rang, and grimaced when he saw the caller was his mother. Apparently she did remember she had a son every once in a while. He was well aware she had her own life now, but was finding it annoying that she only called when she wanted him to do something.

He still couldn't grasp how well he *didn't* know her. His mother was a totally different person than the one he'd known growing up. The one who would carpool him and his friends to school and attend all those activities he had been involved in. The one who would lovingly tuck him into bed at night. The one he thought was not only a fantastic mother but a wonderful wife to his father. She had always seemed so happy. But both he and his father had discovered she had actually been very sad.

"Yes, Mom?"

"Uri, how are you, sweetheart?"

He leaned back against a rail. "I'm fine, Mom, and how are you?"

"Busy. I need a favor from you."

Like there would be any other reason for your call. "What do you need?"

"I know this is short notice, but I need for you to escort Allison Hampton's daughter, Charity, to that dinner and dance Saturday night to raise money for diabetes."

Uriel figured that that must be the same function his father was avoiding this weekend. "Sorry to disappoint you, Mom, but I'm not in Charlotte. I'm out at the lake." Not that he'd have taken snooty Charity Hampton anyway.

"Oh."

He couldn't help wondering if her mind was reliving any memories of how things used to be when she, his father and he would spend time at Cavanaugh Lake.

"Well, have fun at the lake," she said, interrupting his thoughts. "I'll talk with you again soon."

Yes, when you need another favor, he thought before saying, "Goodbye, Mom."

She clicked off the line before returning his goodbye.

He put his phone back in his pocket, thinking he

would make sure he and his mother had a serious conversation, once he returned to Charlotte.

He took a sip of coffee and glanced over at the house next door—specifically at the upstairs bedroom window. Ellie was back, sitting at the window, reading. What in the world was she reading that was still holding her interest? Late yesterday evening after dinner, when he'd come outside to relax, she had been sitting in that chair by the window. And around two in the morning, when he hadn't been able to sleep yet again, he had come outside. From the brightness of the light in the bedroom, he could make out her silhouette behind the drawn curtains, as she sat in that same chair. If she had come outside the house at all yesterday, he hadn't been aware of it.

He checked his watch. He needed to go into Gatlinburg to grab a few supplies, and had volunteered to pick up whatever she needed for her month-long stay as well.

After drinking his coffee, he would head over next door for her list.

Ellie rubbed her hand over her face in frustration, not wanting to believe it. An unfinished manuscript!

Whoever had sent her aunt these pages to edit could possibly be somewhere working on it at this moment. But that wasn't helping Ellie, who had gotten caught up in the couple's passion as well as the love they were both trying to deny.

She wondered if she should call Smoky Mountain Community College and speak to Aphelia Singleton, a librarian who'd worked with her aunt for years. Maybe she would know of someone named Flame Elbam.

The more Ellie thought about it, she had a strong suspicion that Flame Elbam wasn't really the person's true name but a pseudonym. A pseudonym for a woman well-versed in lovemaking. Flame Elbam certainly had a vivid imagination, and Ellie was convinced the person had to be a sexual goddess.

Ellie had gotten pulled into Grant's and Tamara's sexual adventures, to the point where she had put the pages down last night only when she hadn't been able to keep her eyes open any longer. And even after that, she had dreamed about all those sumptuous lovemaking scenes she had read. Her body had gotten unbearably hot, and she had awakened that morning infused with a need that had her wishing, of all things, that she'd had her own Grant.

To make matters worse, Uriel had been back outside, exercising again this morning. As inconspicuously as she could, she had watched him from the window and found herself emerged in all kind of fantasies. It didn't take much to imagine her legs snugly wrapped around the width of his shoulders and her bare breasts coming into contact with the solid wall of his chest.

Unable to deal with further torment, she had forced her gaze away from his flat abs, deciding to let him finish his workout without being spied on. But that didn't stop her from imagining how his sweaty body would feel on top of hers. At sixteen, she used to have visions of Uriel kissing her, and now she was envisioning a whole lot more than mere kisses.

She was halfway down the stairs, headed toward the kitchen, when she heard a knock at the door. She stopped and breathed in deeply. It was as if her thoughts had conjured up Uriel Lassiter.

As she made her way to the door, she couldn't help wondering what he wanted.

After taking a deep breath and pasting a light smile to her lips, she opened the door. "Hello, Uri, what brings you over?"

Uriel figured it couldn't be helped, when his gaze automatically moved from Ellie's face and went straight to her outfit. One thing that hadn't changed over the years was her propensity for wearing those short shorts. They weren't Daisy Dukes, but they were a close cousin. And she looked good in them. Hell, she looked better than good. Seeing her up close was a lot better than seeing her from a distance at the window. Although that nightgown was his favorite outfit on her so far, these shorts were a close second.

"Uri?"

His gaze moved back up to her face and he pulled in a steadying breath. "Yes?" He then watched as she took the tip of her tongue and traced it over her upper lip.

"Is there something you wanted?"

Slowly, he drew in a deep breath, thinking that was a loaded question if ever there was one. Here she stood at the door, looking like someone he would love to crawl back in bed with this morning, and she had the nerve to ask him a question like that?

Inwardly telling himself to get his libido under control, he said, "Today is Tuesday."

When a dumbfounded look appeared on her face he

said, "Remember, I told you I was going into town today. Do you have your list ready?"

"Oh, my gosh, I forgot," she said, slapping the palm of her hand against her forehead. "I've been so busy—"

"Reading."

Ellie inwardly gasped. "How do you know that?"

He shrugged. "I noticed. You've been sitting by the window a lot, and it looked like you were reading."

She nodded, surprised that he had noticed her. Her aunt's home was not in his usual line of vision, which meant he had deliberately looked up at the window.

"Yes, I've been reading," she said. But she had no intention of telling him just what she'd been reading and how he had fit into her fantasies. "I decided to put off going through my aunt's things for a while and enjoy a few lazy days."

He smiled. "There's nothing wrong with that." And then, after a brief pause, he said, "So, is there anything I can get you from town?"

"Yes, but I don't want to hold you up, and—"

"I'm in no hurry. In fact, why not come with me? That way you can get everything you need, and you'll probably see a few things you don't know you need."

She blinked. "You want me to ride into Gatlinburg with you?" she asked in an incredulous tone.

He lifted a brow. "Yes, I believe that was the offer I just made. You have a problem with it?"

Considering the slight frown appearing on his face, she figured he didn't get it, so she said, "No, I don't have a problem with it, but I'd hate for your girlfriend to hear about it and get the wrong idea."

His frown was replaced with a sexy smile. "That's nothing you should concern yourself with, because I don't have a girlfriend."

He studied her features for a moment before asking, "What about you? Is there some serious guy for you that I need to be worried about?"

The only serious guy in her present was Grant Hatteras. The man had been playing with both her and Tamara's emotions for the past eighteen hours. "No, I'm not involved with anyone. I've been too busy with school."

"In that case, there's no reason you and I can't share the same vehicle to go into town and get supplies. Besides, even if we were seriously involved with other people, you and I go way back. We're nothing but friends, right?"

Ellie quickly forced last night's dreams from her mind. Friends didn't do all the things they had done. "Yes, of course. If you don't mind waiting while I grab my purse, it won't take me but a second."

"No problem. I'll wait right here. I don't need to come inside."

She nodded, and then she rushed off to get her purse, leaving him leaning in her doorway.

Chapter 7

"I can't believe you actually eat that stuff."

Ellie couldn't help but smile at how Uriel had scrunched up his face at the asparagus she had placed in the plastic bag. Upon entering the grocery store, they had gotten their own individual carts, but by silent, mutual consent decided to shop together.

"It's good, Uriel. You need to try it."

"I'll pass."

She laughed. "No, honestly, it's all in the way it's prepared. The next time I cook some I'll be sure to share. I think you'll be surprised."

Ellie then glanced at the items accumulating in his basket. She didn't want to sound like a busybody, but she couldn't help but say, "You do know there's a lot of sodium in those microwave dinners, don't you?"

A smile touched the corners of his lips. "Yes, just like I'm sure you know how many fat grams are in that half-gallon of chocolate chip cookie dough ice cream."

Ellie couldn't help but laugh. "Point taken. From now on I'll just worry about what's going into *my* cart."

"Thanks, I'd appreciate that."

Ellie couldn't help but inwardly smile. There was something rather intimate about going grocery shopping with a man. She was getting an idea of the foods he liked and those he didn't like. And she was discovering other detailed personal information, like the brand of soap he used, what shaving cream and that he liked peppermint candy.

"Are you planning on checking out a movie?"

His question reclaimed her thoughts. She looked over at him with a confused expression. "You've got a lot of stuff in your grocery cart that's symbolic of movie night," he explained.

She couldn't help but smile when she saw she did indeed. In addition to the microwave popcorn, she had gotten a bag of gummy bears, a big bag of nachos and a canister of the melted cheese. Then there were the sodas as well as the wine coolers.

"No, I hadn't thought about it actually. These are things I figured I'd treat myself to at least some time during the month I'm here. I couldn't tell you the last time I watched a movie or went to one. Schoolwork came first."

A look of disbelief appeared on his face. "You mean you haven't seen anything?"

He then went through a list of recent movies.

"Afraid not."

"Then I'm going to have to fix that. You decide on the night, and then you do the popcorn and wine coolers and I'll bring the movie. I have a collection of DVDs I've brought to the lake with me. We'll make it a movie night."

Ellie reached for a bottle of Tabasco sauce, refusing to look over at Uriel. She wondered if he realized what he'd just suggested sounded like a date. Probably not, she figured as they kept walking, sharing space in the aisle. After all, he had defined their relationship as being nothing more than friends.

A half hour later, with their carts fully loaded, they had left the store but not before several people who'd recognized her as Mable Weston's niece approached her to convey their condolences.

Uriel was very organized when he arranged everything in his SUV, making sure her items were in the back so they could be removed first. "Are there any other stops you'd like to make before we head back home?" he asked.

She wondered if he'd noticed that he'd asked the question as if they were a married couple who'd just done grocery stopping together and was returning to the same house. "No, I'm fine."

"Do you mind if I stop by Logan's hardware store? I need to get some more hooks."

"No, I don't mind."

After making the stop at the hardware store, Uriel suggested they grab something to eat at one of the diners in town, since it was so close to lunchtime.

"What about your frozen dinners?" she decided to ask. "And the ice cream?"

"Thanks for reminding me. We'll get our orders to go," he said, as he pulled into Buddy's Diner.

As she resettled in the truck, she couldn't help but appreciate how easily they seemed to get along. They teased each other mercilessly about their purchases, but it had all been in fun.

"Next time we decide to ride into town together to pick up a few things, we'll grab lunch before hitting the grocery store," he said, glancing over at her and smiling.

She didn't say anything, just let the words flow between them while fighting the flutter in the bottom of her stomach. That was the third time today he'd said something that made them seem like a couple. Were they words spoken between friends with no hidden meaning? Or was he throwing around some type of hints of possibly something more?

When Ellie snapped her seat belt in place she decided not to put more stock into something that really wasn't there. The little innuendos Grant would occasionally say to Tamara were getting to her, making her dissect Uriel's every word for some hidden meaning. She had to pull her mind out of fantasy land and back into reality. They were not the hero and heroine in a hot and steamy romance novel. The man sitting beside her was Uriel and she was Ellie. And the conversation they had been exchanging was merely words spoken between friends. Nothing more.

As he tightened his grip on the steering wheel, Uriel muttered a curse that was too low for Ellie to hear. What was with all these slip-ups he was making?

Damn. He was getting too comfy with Ellie. Letting down the guard he usually kept up with most women. It could possibly be the result of his dream last night and the visions that keep popping up in his head. In his dream, she had been sitting cross-legged in the middle of his bed. Naked. And waiting for him to tear off his clothes and join her there. The dream had been as erotic as any dream could get, and before he could join her on the bed, something had awakened him.

Unable to resurrect the dream, and with no sleep in sight, he got up at 2:00 a.m. for the second straight night and had gone outside to sit on the porch. He had fervently hoped he would be lucky and she'd be standing at the window, half-naked again, with her glass of wine. To his disappointment, she hadn't been.

He gripped the steering wheel even tighter, and kept his focus on the road while trying to come up with one good reason he shouldn't pursue a relationship with Ellie. She was no longer a minor, but a full-grown woman who could make her own decisions. He was attracted to her bigtime. She didn't have a significant other and neither did he.

Something else he needed to consider was that their families knew each other, which in a way wasn't a bad thing, but it wasn't necessarily a good thing, either. She already knew more about him than he would have shared with a woman, especially the situation with his parents. He was sure she had heard the story about his mother and her boy-toy. Hadn't practically everybody?

He loosened his hold on the steering wheel when the thought of an affair with Ellie began to take shape in his mind. A month was long enough to indulge in an affair. Hell, that was longer than most of his affairs.

"Are you still into photography?"

Her question made him glance quickly over at her, before returning his gaze to the road. He was surprised she remembered that. "Not as much as I used to be," he responded. "That was something I outgrew, especially when I found out that I would be responsible for buying my own film. Too much out of my allowance. So I got another interest that didn't cost as much."

When he came to a stop sign he glanced over at her. "What about you? Did you ever write your book?"

Ellie blinked, and then she couldn't help but chuckle when she remembered. Gosh, how long ago had that been? She was probably no more than twelve that one summer when she'd decided after reading a Nancy Drew Mystery that she would pen one of her own. She had interviewed everyone for her book, including him, and she hadn't gotten past the first chapter when she decided writing was too much work.

"No, but when I got to college I did enough writing, with all those term papers."

He nodded. "So, are you through with school, or will you go ahead and get your PhD, like your parents?" Both of her parents were college professors.

"I've had enough of school. I'm hoping my entrance into the workforce this time is better than the last. I only had the job a year before I got laid off. That's why I went to grad school."

"What is your field of study?"

"Finance."

As he rounded the lake, he said. “Hopefully, with the economy improving, you won’t have a problem finding a job and keeping it.”

“I hope not.”

The SUV came to a stop in front of her house. “I’ll help you get your stuff inside. Just unlock the door for me.”

“Thanks.”

While he unloaded her purchases, she quickly walked ahead, unlocked the door and pushed it open. When he strolled by her she got a whiff of his after-shave, the same one that had played havoc on her senses during the ride home. The same one that reminded her of what a strong male he was—not that she could forget.

She followed him into the kitchen where he sat her bags on the table. “I’ll go get the rest of the stuff,” he said, before walking out. She began going through the bags, immediately taking out the ice cream to place in the freezer. She was putting away items in the pantry when he returned after a couple of trips.

“Okay, that’s everything that’s yours.”

Ellie moved away from the pantry to where he’d placed the other bags on the table. She hadn’t realized she bought so much. “Thanks, Uri, for everything.”

“No problem. I’ll check you out later.”

Uriel turned to leave, almost got to her kitchen door when something stopped him. It could have been a number of things. It could have been the dream he’d had last night, or the memory of the kiss they’d shared all those years ago that had been playing on his mind a lot lately. It could be something as simple as the fact that he was a man and she was a woman, and the chemistry between them had been more potent today than ever. It could have been any one of those things or all of them.

She noticed she hadn't heard the back door close behind him, so she glanced over—at *him*. Met his gaze.

He stood there with his focus directly on her, while trying to figure out what there was about her that made him want to strip her naked, right here in this kitchen, but not before he got to taste her again, to see if the flavor of her mouth had changed, and to see if she could still work her tongue like she had before.

His eyes slowly shifted lower to her breasts. He pulled in a choppy breath when he saw her nipples start to harden right before his eyes. Hell, if just a look could do that to her, he wondered what would happen if he were to touch her, taste her kiss.

He could feel his own eyes darkening with heat, and he knew the moment she saw it as well. She continued to hold his gaze, then asked, "Is there something else?"

He couldn't help the smile that touched his lips. She could ask the damnedest questions. This time he would give her an answer, and he hoped she was ready for his response. "Yes, there is something else," he said, walking back toward her.

He came to a stop in front of her, and because of their difference in heights, she tilted her head back to look up at him. He figured, at some point she must have figured what this was about. He had to kiss her. For no other purpose than to appease the curiosity between them, harness this sensuous pull, take control of the sexual attraction. And that was precisely what he intended to do. Now.

He lowered his head toward hers, and when their mouths were mere inches apart, when he could feel the heat off her lips radiating toward his, he paused. He was giving her a chance to pull back, resist what he was about to do. But when she darted her tongue out of her mouth to moisten her top lip, he decided it was too damn late.

Before she could put her tongue back, he sank his mouth down on hers, taking it all. He immediately grabbed hold of her tongue with his and began sucking on it, as he had in his dream. And when she moaned deep in her throat and wrapped her arms around his neck, every nerve in his body began to flicker, his erection began to throb. To let her know just how aroused he was, he pulled her closer into his arms, and pressed the lower part of his body to hers.

It didn't take long for Uriel to see that this kind of kiss could turn dangerous, especially if he listened to what his aroused body was begging him to do. It wouldn't take much for him to push everything off the table and take her there. Hell, taking her against the refrigerator sounded even better. The bottom line was that he wanted to take her. Somewhere. Now. Standing up in this very spot would even work. All he had to do was pull her shorts and panties down, undo his zipper and get to work.

But he realized that the first time he entered her body he wouldn't want it to be a quickie. He would want to savor the moment, enjoy the buildup. So, until that time came, he would enjoy this, the meshing of their tongues, while he got aroused by her taste. It was nothing like he remembered. The flavor was more intense, her tongue more controlled.

The kiss was everything he'd known it would be, everything he'd imagined as well as dreamt about. Every lick sent sensations rushing all the way to his toes, had blood rushing through his veins and made something in the pit of his stomach stir to the point where he couldn't help but deepen the kiss, pull her closer to his body and begin backing her up toward the refrigerator after all.

The moment Ellie felt the refrigerator against her back she pulled her mouth free from Uriel's and whispered, "Wow."

Her mind began reeling, her pulse was racing and tingling sensations were having a serious confrontation between her legs. She gazed into Uriel's eyes that were so close to hers. He hadn't backed up any. It was as if he just wanted her to get her breath, since he wasn't quite through with her yet.

The intensity in the gaze holding hers said as much. She could only stare back, transfixed. Pressed against the fridge, she should have felt trapped. Instead, she felt provoked into seeing just how far he would take this.

Ellie pulled in a deep breath. She needed to think, and then quickly decided that, no, she didn't. What she seriously needed to do was play this out, see where it would go and put a stop to it if it became too much. This was Uriel. He wouldn't force her to do anything she didn't want to do. Although he had initiated the kiss, she hadn't fought it, because she had needed it. Seeing him naked, and then seeing him every morning working out, had been too much for a woman who hadn't had sex in quite a while to handle.

Staring into his face, she knew he was waiting for her to make the next move, since she'd been the one to end the kiss. She detected patience in him and knew he would wait, give her time to make up her mind. But she also understood, and very clearly, that if the decision didn't go the way he wanted, his untamed side, the one she detected he possessed, had no qualms about using seduction to sway her to what he wanted. The very thought of being seduced by him had her drawing in another breath, just seconds before she leaned closer and touched her mouth to his again.

And he took things from there—immediately deepening the kiss, to make up for lost time. In a way, she wasn't the least bit surprised or shocked by the intensity of the kiss. He was kissing her with the confidence of a man who knew exactly what he was doing. A man who knew what he wanted, with no qualms about getting it, but making sure he enjoyed it in the process. A man who knew how to combine an ample measure of warmth with his hunger, an enormous amount of sensuality with his greed, and who had the ability to ignite passion around with a force that made her weak in the knees.

When she felt his hands move to the waistband of her shorts, felt his fingers inch lower, tracing a path past her panties, seeking hot bounty, she pulled her mouth away. "We have to stop."

His brow lifted with an arrogance that she found totally captivating. "Do we?"

The man was too much. "I think we'd better," she whispered.

He held her gaze. "You think so?"

"Don't you?" she countered.

His response was quick. "No."

She couldn't do anything but drop her head to his chest and mumble against his shirt. "You're not helping matters."

"Am I supposed to?"

She lifted her head, gazed into his eyes and tried smiling reassuringly. "That would really help."

"All right."

He then pulled his hands from within her shorts, but he didn't move away, just backed up. A little. A quiver slid down her spine at the intensity of the gaze holding hers. And she knew he was in a waiting mode, to see what she would do or say next.

"How did we go from just friends to this?" she heard herself asking, while still trying to force air through her lungs. She had never been kissed that way. Had never participated in anything so intense that it nearly snapped her senses.

He shrugged and then said, "I've wanted you pretty bad ever since I saw you that night at the window."

She lifted a brow. "You saw me at the window one night?" At his nod, she asked. "When?"

"A few nights ago. Evidently, you couldn't sleep and neither could I—which has been happening a lot lately—so I thought I'd sit on the back porch a while. The lights came on in your bedroom and sometime later you came to the window to look out at the lake. You were wearing a very short and ultrasexy nightie. I couldn't see everything, but I saw enough."

Ellie swallowed deeply. Yes, she could tell by the look in his eyes that he had seen enough. She remembered that night. She hadn't been able to sleep and had drunk more wine than she really should have. "I didn't know you were watching."

"I know. It was dark, and not once did you glance over at the porch. You just stood there staring at the lake. I could understand why. It was a beautiful night and a full moon was in the sky. You were satisfied with just staring at the lake and I was satisfied with just staring at you. I've been back every night since then, feeling restless, edgy, but you haven't been back."

"And?" she asked, wondering why he was telling her this.

"And there's nothing else to tell. Like I said, you hadn't been back and I've been fine at fighting the temptation."

Until today, evidently, she figured. He had been fine until today, when they had gone into Gatlinburg together. "And what made you kiss me?" she asked him, hoping he would answer, since he seemed not to mind talking about it.

"That day at the lake, when you took your friend up on that dare, I had enjoyed kissing you. I was curious to see if I would enjoy kissing you now. And today I just couldn't leave until I found out."

"And?" she asked, as she relaxed back against the refrigerator.

His brows rose. "I enjoyed it. Couldn't you tell?"

Yes, she had been able to tell, but then it definitely had been a mutual exchange. "I need to finish putting things away," she said, deciding it was time for her to rein in her senses and for him to do the same with his.

An affair would be a waste of their time, because it

would be an affair that went nowhere. He wasn't into long-term, and she'd figured whenever she did get back into the dating scene, that she would be. She never intended to spend the rest of her life alone, without a special man in it, as her aunt had done. She wanted to marry, have children. She wanted the white picket fence and the house that it surrounded. She had a feeling he didn't.

"All right, I'll let you call time out for now," he said, taking another step back, giving her a lot of space.

"Excuse me?" She must not have heard him correctly.

"I know what's probably going through your mind right now. You're probably wondering if an affair—a short-term affair—with me is worth it. We'll be here for a little less than thirty days, so the way I see it, we could either be bored to death or we can really enjoy each other's company."

She lifted her chin. "What makes you think I'd be bored?"

"Just a guess."

Unfortunately, Ellie thought, he had probably guessed right. If she had the rest of that manuscript to read, then she would have had something to look forward to doing for the next couple of days. And packing her aunt's things would keep her busy, but only for a while. But no matter how you looked at it, indulging in an affair with Uriel Lassiter was too much to think about. She wasn't sure she could handle him. The man had more sexual energy than any man she knew. His kiss had confirmed that.

"I propose we have a summer fling, Ellie. At the end of the summer, when we leave here, you will go your way and I'll go mine. No attachments. No follow-up visits or phone calls. No cards in the mail during the holidays, nor any getting together for an Easter feast. And when we do see each other again we'll be friends. Former lovers who'll always be nothing more than friends."

He paused and she knew he was letting his words sink in. "I'll give you a few days to think about it," he said, backing up.

The lines around his lips eased into a smile. "You know where I'll be once you've made a decision."

She didn't say anything, just stood there and stared at him and then stared at the door when he left.

Chapter 8

Uriel pulled the dinner out of the microwave and placed it on the table before moving to the refrigerator to pull out a can of soda. It was a nice day, and he had thought about eating outside on the porch but changed his mind. There was no way he could sit on his porch and not look over to where he knew Ellie was.

It had been two days since he had kissed her. He'd told her that he'd give her a few days to consider an affair between them, but hadn't really expected for her to take all this time. What was there to think about? They were attracted to each other. There was strong sexual chemistry. They had enjoyed kissing each other, which meant sleeping together would be enjoyable as well.

That night, when he'd gone to bed and thought about it, he had figured out why she was holding back. Her parents' marriage was a good role model for her to go by, and she wanted the same thing they had. So she was holding out for marriage and was not into casual affairs.

Sitting down at the table, he bowed his head and said grace before digging into his meal. He couldn't help but grin when he recalled how she'd warned him about the amount of sodium in his microwave dinner. He would have to admit that he had enjoyed going grocery shopping with her that day, the first time with any woman. For some reason it had seemed natural to be with her in that store.

He wondered how long she would stay locked up in that house. Was she deliberately avoiding him or was she actually busy packing up Ms. Mable's belongings? He had seen the Salvation Army truck over there yesterday. Still, the last two days had been nice ones, so she should have been outside enjoying them.

He was tempted to go over there once or twice, but had changed his mind. But that hadn't stopped him waking up around two every morning, easing onto the porch and sitting in the dark, hoping that he would catch a glimpse of her standing by the window again. He hadn't. In fact, the light in her bedroom never came on, which meant she was getting a good night's sleep, even if he wasn't.

For the last two days, he'd been lucky with his fishing rod and had caught enough for a fish fry this weekend. He wondered if Ellie would be interested in joining him. No matter what her ultimate decision would be about an affair, they would remain friends, although it was hard to be friends with a woman you wanted to take to bed.

At that moment he heard a car door slam, and wondered if someone was paying him a visit. Four of his godbrothers were here in the States and knew where they could find him, but he doubted they would come looking for him.

He stood and walked through the kitchen to the living room, to glance out the window. The car he'd heard was actually next door. Someone was paying Ellie a visit, and it was a man. He frowned. She'd said she was not involved with anyone, so who would come to the lake to see her?

Uriel squinted his eyes against the sun and saw it was Daniel Altman, the man who had been Ms. Mable's attorney for years. Evidently, the older man needed to finalize a few things with Ellie regarding her aunt's estate.

Satisfied this was nothing but a business call, he headed back to the kitchen to finish his dinner, refusing to admit that for a moment, his deep, dark thoughts had been those of a jealous man.

"I wasn't aware my aunt's estate encompassed all of this," Ellie said, after Daniel Altman had gone over everything with her.

The older gentleman smiled. "Yes, your aunt invested wisely, and that's a good thing, considering how the stock market has taken a beating. Other than the money she's set aside for that scholarship at Smoky Mountain Community College, everything of hers is now yours."

The man then shifted uneasily in his chair. "Your aunt was a very private person, and there was one business deal she was involved with where she preferred that any correspondence relating to it come directly to me. I would deliver the mail to her."

Ellie lifted a brow. "Why?"

"I believe this letter will explain everything. It's addressed to you, and she would update it every so often to try and keep it current," he said, handing Ellie the sealed envelope.

He glanced at his watch and said, "I need to leave now, but if you have questions about any of this, just give me a call tomorrow."

He paused a moment and then said, "I'll be retiring from practicing law in a few months and will be moving to Florida. I bought a small place in Ocala. I'm getting too old to handle the harsh winters here any longer."

She smiled. "I am happy for you, Mr. Altman," she said, getting up off the sofa to walk him to the door. "I'm going to miss seeing you around."

Her aunt had left her enough money to open her own financial consulting company, and she was considering doing just that, and to work from here at Cavanaugh Lake.

Mr. Altman turned to her and said softly, "I considered your aunt a close friend as well as a good client, and there was nothing I wouldn't do for her."

Ellie's smile brightened. "Thanks, Mr. Altman. And I believe I speak for my parents as well as myself when I say that we have appreciated your friendship and loyalty to my aunt over the years. She always spoke highly of you and indicated you always provided outstanding service."

She thought she actually saw the man blush when he said, "I did my best." He then quickly opened the door and left.

Ellie stood at the door and watched him hurry to his car, and couldn't help wondering what that was all about. For some reason, she thought Mr. Altman had begun acting rather strange. For someone who was about to retire, he didn't seem all that happy about it. In fact, if she didn't know better, she'd think he was sad. Shrugging her shoulders, she went back into the living room to read the letter her aunt had left for her. It had been dated a month before she died.

To my beautiful niece,

If you're reading this letter, it means I am no longer with you. There's a lot I shared with you and some things I didn't share. There are some things I could never bring myself to talk to you about. I admit I took the coward's way out, but after reading this letter I hope you will understand.

A few years ago I did something that I thought I would never do, and that was to fall in love.

Ellie nearly dropped the letter. Aunt Mable? In love? She blinked and reread that passage of the letter again, to make sure she had read it correctly, and when she saw she had, she quickly read on.

He was a widower and we talked about getting married, but I had been alone for so long, all I really needed was companionship, and he provided that for me; and with this being such a small town, and not wanting our relationship to be dictated by traditional ideals, we preferred being discreet and keeping our business to ourselves. Anyway, I've always wanted to write, and he encouraged me to do so. I wanted to write a love story, and after much encouragement I sat down and started on it.

Ellie was feeling the hairs on the back of her neck stand up, and she had a strong suspicion what her aunt was about to tell her.

I'm hoping by the time you read this I've gotten published. That is my dream. That is my goal. A publisher out of Texas has purchased my first story. They loved it! They gave me an advance, and understanding that I was a new writer, they were gracious enough to give me a year to complete it. I am attaching my agent's card to this letter. Her name is Lauren Poole. She's been a jewel to work with and the book has been a jewel to write. The manuscript is my baby. I'm entrusting it into your care if something were to happen me. I'm writing under the name of Flame Elbam. Note that Elbam *is* Mable *spelled backward. That's kind of cute, don't you think? I'm hoping by the time you read this letter, I would have finished plenty of novels.*

Always know that I love you and I hope that one day you will share the kind of love that I have shared in the last few years. Don't wait as long as I did to find love. There is nothing more precious for a woman than sharing the love of a man that she can call hers.

Many kisses and much love,

Aunt Mable

Ellie couldn't fight back the tears that fell from her eyes. It was hard to believe. Her aunt, who had never married, had become Flame Elbam and had penned a beautiful romance filled with more passion than Ellie could ever imagine.

It was a story she hadn't finished, and now, with her passing, it would be a story that would never get finished.

Ellie shook her head at the cruelty of it all. She removed the agent's business card denoting a New York address. Ellie would call her tomorrow, to see if there was something that could be done. Maybe a ghost writer could finish the final chapters. Surely, the publisher could find someone to do that.

And if that option wouldn't be acceptable to the publisher, Ellie would make sure the company got back every dime of its advance.

She then wondered about the man who had been her aunt's lover, and when she recalled the artwork hanging on her aunt's bedroom wall, it all made sense.

To Flame, with all my love. D.

Her aunt never said who her lover was, but Ellie had a strong suspicion that the man who'd given her aunt the risqué painting and the man who had delivered the papers to Ellie this afternoon were one and the same, although she would not have thought so in a hundred years. But that just proved you couldn't discount what people did in their bedrooms. In order for her aunt to write about such passion, she'd had to experience it at the hands of Daniel Altman.

Ellie stood. She would call Lauren Poole, and whatever it took, she would make sure the manuscript her aunt considered "her baby" got published.

"No, Xavier, I really mean it. The fish have really been biting the last few days," Uriel said to one of his godbrothers, the only one who also lived in Charlotte.

"If I didn't have plans for this weekend, I'd be tempted to head your way," Xavier was saying.

Uriel nodded. He didn't have to figure what kind of plans Xavier had. Like him, all of his godbrothers were Bachelors in Demand, who had no desire to marry anytime soon—or ever.

He and Xavier talked for another fifteen minutes or so, and then they ended the call. Uriel had been enjoying a movie every night this week, and had been getting in bed before ten. That would be just fine if he slept through the night, but he did not.

Tomorrow, after his early morning workout, he would start cleaning all the fish he'd caught, and then, if Ellie still hadn't made contact with him by Saturday, he planned to go over there and have a talk with her. She'd made it pretty clear she did not want to indulge in an affair, and that was fine, although he wished otherwise.

He noticed Daniel Altman hadn't stayed long, and now the house was completely dark. The lights in the upstairs bedroom were off, which meant she'd gone to bed and was probably getting a good night's sleep.

He decided to take a shower and then check out the sports station to see what was happening there. He didn't want to admit it, but he missed seeing Ellie over the past couple of days and hoped he got a chance to see her tomorrow.

Ellie tossed around in the small bed, trying to get comfortable. Instead of sleeping in her aunt's room for the past two nights, she had slept in the guest room, which was located on the opposite side of the house. That way, Uriel wouldn't know when she turned on a bedroom light.

She hadn't wanted him to know, especially that first night, that the kiss they'd shared had definitely made an impact on her. She knew he was still waiting on a decision regarding an affair, but she didn't have one to give him. She didn't want a short-term affair and he didn't want a long-term one. A relationship would not work out between them, because they wanted different things in life. She had tried avoiding him, but eventually she would have to go outside.

And when she did she would see him. She remembered the kiss that nearly scorched her toes. The kiss that still could render her breathless, just thinking about it.

To keep Uriel off her mind, she had been able to pack up a lot of her aunt's belongings over the past two days and had everything ready for the Salvation Army truck when it arrived. More than once, she had been tempted to call Uriel over to handle a big box for her, but had quickly changed her mind, not wanting to give him any ideas. He had pretty much told her what he was looking for in a relationship, and it wasn't the same thing she wanted. He wanted a summer fling that would last while the two of them were here on the lake. But she couldn't risk that because when it was over, her heart would break.

She'd had this crush on Uriel for years—one that had lasted through her adolescent years and all through her teens. Even after that incident that day on the pier, when he had walked off from her with anger in his eyes at what she'd done, she had still loved him and had come to the lake each year after that for five straight years, hoping the anger within him would have subsided. She had even tried calling him a few months later at college to apologize, after getting his cell number from his father, only to get cold feet and hang up when she'd heard his voice. When it became apparent to her that he would keep his word and not come to the lake while she was there, she had stopped coming.

And now, after ten years, they were both back at the lake; they were adults who were attracted to each other, though for her it went a little farther than that. A part of her still loved Uriel and would always love him. For some women, teen crushes faded over time; but not for her, which was why she could not consider a fling with him. She would need something more lasting than that.

Chapter 9

"Okay, El, start at the beginning."

Ellie rolled her eyes as she slumped down in her favorite chair. She glanced out the window. Uriel was in the middle of his workout. It was close to nine, which meant he'd gotten a late start this morning for some reason. She'd had a sleepless night, and she couldn't help wondering what his excuse was.

She tried turning her attention away from Uriel and back to her conversation with Darcy. She had meant to call her aunt's agent first thing this morning, but before she could do so she had gotten a call from Darcy, who in a very excited voice had told her about a job offer she'd gotten with the City of New York.

Ellie was happy for her friend and knew it had been Darcy's lifelong dream to live in the Big Apple. Darcy worked hard and was good at what she did as a city planner. Minneapolis's loss was now Manhattan's gain. After going through all the congratulations and deciding when the two of them could get together to celebrate, Ellie, needing someone to talk to, and had unloaded on Darcy, telling her all the things that had happened over the past two days, namely Uriel wanting a summer fling and her aunt being, of all things, a romance author of erotica fiction.

"Just what part didn't you get, Darcy?" she finally asked.

"Both."

Ellie pulled in a deep breath as she went through everything again. From her time spent in Gatlinburg with Uriel to their heated kiss, and then his proposal that they have a summer fling, all the way to the letter her aunt had left with her attorney. Surprisingly, Darcy just listened and let her talk without any interruptions.

When she was finished Darcy had her turn. "Okay, let's take one issue at a time. I understand about you and Uriel. You've been hooked on the guy forever, and you're not bad-looking, so quite naturally he would come on to you. Personally, I expected it. And if you recall, that day the two of you kissed on the pier, he was enjoying it. He only got pissed off because I interrupted things. You were too busy kissing him back to notice that he was attacking your mouth just as much as you were attacking his."

Darcy paused briefly, then continued. "Now fast-forward to present day. Most men his age aren't ready for commitment. In a way, I wish Harold hadn't assumed that he was. It would have saved me a lot of misery. I applaud a guy who won't marry until he feels that he's ready. And in the meantime, do you really expect him to twiddle his thumb and lay off women until then? Come on, El, that's not how it works. I read plenty of romance novels, but this here is the real world. Men prefer affairs, and believe it or not, some women do, too. Things are less complicated that way."

"Are you saying that maybe I *should* consider having a summer fling with Uriel?"

"It's your decision, Ellie, and I can't help but admire Uriel for giving you the time to make it. Most men, especially one our age, would use this time to seduce you into one. From what you've said, Uriel has kept his distance, giving you a chance to think straight, without him being around. In other words, he hasn't sought you out."

Ellie gnawed on her bottom lip, deciding it wasn't necessary to tell Darcy that it had been the other way around. She had sought him out, without him knowing she'd done so. Uriel had no idea that she watched him work out every morning or that she would often watch him fish from the pier.

"Now, with this issue involving your aunt. I can't believe she actually penned a romance novel. And one with love scenes. How hot were they?"

Darcy's words pulled Ellie's thoughts back in. "They were hot. Actually a bit erotic. But the love scenes fit the story."

"So you enjoyed it, hmm?"

Ellie knew what Darcy was getting at. "Okay, I did

enjoy it. It was different from what I've been reading, so I was quickly pulled in. After the first chapter, I knew it was more than that. It was truly a well-written story. I hate that the manuscript didn't get finished."

"So, what are you going to do about that?" Darcy asked.

"There's nothing I can do but contact her agent to let her know Aunt Mable passed on, and to find out how much of an advance she received so that I can return it to her."

Darcy didn't say anything for a moment, and then said, "You know there is another option, don't you?"

Ellie raised her brow. "And what option is that?"

"You can finish it."

"What!" Ellie exclaimed, jumping out the chair. "Are you nuts, Darcy? There's no way I can finish that book. First of all, I know nothing about writing a novel, and then, did you miss the part when I said that it's a *romance* book, with plenty of sensuality and passion—two things I know nothing about?"

"Calm down, Ellie, and listen to me for a second, because I think you're wrong. You *can* finish it. I think you owe it to your aunt to do so. You read what she wrote in that letter. It was her dream to get that book published. And you said there're only a few chapters left. The only thing you need is to get romantically and sexually inspired, and we both know the person who can serve as some real-life inspiration."

Ellie frowned. "Don't even think it."

"Sorry, too late. I'm already thinking it. I think it's perfect. If the book is that good, then you owe it to Ms. Mable to finish it, even if it means that summer fling with Uriel to get inspired, to feel how sensuality and passion works hand-in-hand."

Ellie rolled her eyes while shaking her head. "That doesn't mean I would able to finish that book, Darcy. I'm not a writer."

"But you are your aunt's niece. Her favorite niece. Her only niece. You even got her name, Ellie *Mable* Weston. So, in essence, a Mable Weston *would* have written the book."

"Jeesh" was the only comment Ellie could make, not believing Darcy's logic.

"And I believe, once you start writing, that Ms. Mable will also inspire you with the right words to say," Darcy tacked on.

Ellie didn't say anything for a moment. Would her aunt do that? She didn't necessarily believe in the paranormal, but if it was possible, her aunt would find a way to reach her. "But what about Uriel? He would never go along with being used that way," she said.

"You're talking nonsense now, Ellie. The man asked you to indulge in a summer fling. It's all about sex, girl, so get real. If you agree to it, do you think he'd care one iota that he's inspiring you or that you're doing research for a book? In fact, why even bother telling him? The fewer details men know about certain things, the better. Uriel thinks your aunt was a sweet old lady. Do you really want him to know she was a hot tamale?"

"Darcy!"

"Sorry, but you know what I mean. Think about my suggestion. Your aunt was given until the end of the year to finish that book. If I were you, I would finish it and turn it in as soon as possible. If the agent thinks it doesn't work she will let you know it. If it flows and turns out to be a good book, like I know it will be, at least there will be one book on the shelf written by Flame Elbam, and no one will know the truth but me and you. And if the agent wants another book, we can tell her then that your aunt passed away. We don't have to tell her when."

Ellie eased back in the chair and closed her eyes. Sometimes she actually thought that Darcy was in the wrong profession. She could plot deception too easily. "I need to think about this."

"Then think about it, and if you decide to let Uriel be your inspiration, all you have to do is let him know you'll agree to that summer fling. You don't have to give him a reason. And then, who knows? In the midst of it all, Uriel just might figure out that you're the best thing to ever happen to him, and you'll cure him of his commitment phobia."

Ellie used the rest of that day to pack up some more of Aunt Mable's things. Around noon, she had stopped for lunch, and later that day she took a break for dinner. It was only later, when the sun had finally gone down that she decided to call it a day, take a shower and relax.

She sat downstairs on the sofa with a glass of wine and her aunt's letter and unfinished manuscript, to ponder her options. She hadn't called Lauren Poole today, deciding to give Darcy's suggestions some thought first. Was finishing this manuscript something she could actually pull off?

She took a sip of wine and then reread her aunt's letter. Afterward, she placed it aside and picked up the manuscript and began reading it again.

The room was quiet, and reading her aunt's words a second time was just as exhilarating as the first. After she finished the first chapter, she took another sip of wine and smiled to herself. Darcy really had a lot of confidence in her abilities, if she thought she could just come in and finish this story without a reader recognizing it hadn't been written by the same person. But then, as she continued reading, she had thoughts and ideas on just how she would want the book to continue and then to conclude. But would those have been her aunt's thoughts and plans for her hero and heroine?

Ellie lifted her eyes from the manuscript and sighed deeply. And what about those hot and steamy lovemaking scenes, where sparks were flying off the pages? It had been years since she'd actually shared a bed with a man, and even then things had been kind of rushed each time. Could she actually write the love scenes after obtaining some real-life inspiration?

In a way, Darcy was right. Uriel had asked her to indulge in a summer fling. If she decided to go along with it, did he have to know her motives for doing so? Darcy was probably right in thinking that he wouldn't care. Especially since he'd made it known he was not interested in anything long-term. They would be former lovers who were nothing more than friends. Those had been his words, and not hers.

She took a sip of her wine and continued reading. A short while later she lifted her gaze from the page to draw in a deep breath. With each lovemaking scene she could actually feel when Grant stroked Tamara's skin. When he whispered words into Tamara's ear he might as well be whispering them into hers, as well.

Ellie loosened the two top buttons of her blouse, then shifted positions when the cotton material of her shorts suddenly seemed sensitive against her skin. She was beginning to feel hot. Aroused. Sexually deprived. Her lips curved. Maybe she was enjoying too much wine tonight. Too much wine and not enough man.

At least, not a *certain* man.

She could actually admit, in all honesty, that she'd only really been kissed twice in her life. And both times by Uriel. Kisses she'd receive from other men didn't even come close. For one, long heartbeat of a moment, she stared into space as she remembered the kiss that had taken place a few days ago in her kitchen. She recalled how her back had felt pressed against the refrigerator while a very hungry mouth had devoured hers.

There was no doubt in her mind that Uriel was all the real-life inspiration she would need, and that he was not only capable of stimulating her body to where she would probably not only put sexy words on paper, but talk all kinds of stuff in her sleep. Especially if the size of the erection she'd felt that day, pressing hard against her, was anything to go by. No doubt he would teach her a lot, inspire her plenty and leave her wanting more, only to deliver time and time again.

The thought was tempting, so much so, in fact, that she could feel her inner muscles quivering, the area between her legs tingling and the heat invading her body and taking over her common sense.

Was this the opportunity that she had been waiting for all her life, at least since the time she'd decided she would love Uriel forever, marry him one day and have his babies? Even then, those had been the dreams of a teenager who didn't know, hadn't a clue just what she'd been hoping for. Now she knew.

She sighed deeply and placed the rubber band back around the unfinished pages, placed the letter on top to put the items away. Her decision had been made. She would be the one to finish her aunt's manuscript. Darcy was right. Aunt Mable would want it that way. She would pay Uriel a visit tomorrow and tell him that she would indulge in an affair with him.

Picking up her items, she carefully balanced everything in her hands as she climbed the stairs. She turned on the light in her aunt's room and went to the desk, placed the manuscript and letter in a drawer and locked it. She then glanced over at the clock. It was close to 2:00 a.m. Had she been reading that long?

She turned off the light to leave the room, when her gaze traveled to the window. She then recalled what Uriel had said about not being able to sleep sometimes at night, and that one of those nights he had been outside, sitting on the porch, and had seen her at the window, wearing a nightie.

Was he outside now, sitting on the porch? Restless, edgy, possibly even a bit horny? What would he do if she appeared at the window, pretended she didn't know he was there and started removing her clothes, piece by piece? Feeling naughty, wild, with a burst of erratic hormones she hadn't realized she had until now, she turned the light back on and moved toward the window.

She might wait and give Uriel her decision tomorrow, but she intended to send him a very intimate message tonight.

Uriel stood at the kitchen sink and wet his hands to wipe across his face. He felt hot, filled with a fiery sensation, a primal urge, that even sleeping in the nude hadn't eased. So he had slipped into a pair of shorts to come downstairs. He glanced at the clock on the stove. It was two in the morning. He should have guessed. This restlessness, edginess, was becoming a nightly thing around this time.

As usual, he'd had his dreams, and as usual, he had awakened just seconds before joining his body with Ellie's. Would there ever be a dream when he would complete the act and relieve himself of his misery? When would he feel what it would be like to be inside her body, have her inner muscles clench him tightly, milk him dry? He would have to settle for a dream, since it seemed she had decided an affair with him was not what she wanted. This had been day three, and he had pretty much gotten her message loud and clear. There would be no summer fling between them.

In the morning he would go over there, give her some of the fish he'd caught and offer to fry them for her. He would then tell her that he'd accepted her decision and, as nothing more than friends, they could at least enjoy each other's company for the rest of the summer.

But during the wee hours of the night, while alone in his bed, he would continue to dream about her and to do to her in his fantasies what she refused to let him do in reality.

He crossed the darkened kitchen and headed for the back door, opened it and stepped outside. It was hot, but the cool breeze from the lake was swirling around, spraying a light mist on his naked chest. The moment he sat down in the swing he glanced next door, and his pulse rate accelerated when he saw the light was on in Ms. Mable's bedroom. The first time in three days.

He sat there with his gaze transfixed to the window. He had told her he'd sometimes sit out here at night and look over at the window. For that reason alone, Ellie would probably not come close to the window, knowing there was a possibility that he would be watching.

But still, that didn't stop him from sitting and staring. He figured, sitting out here, being hopeful, was a hell of a lot better going back to bed and dreaming and being disappointed.

The light went out and he mentally swore, followed by the muttering of a few choice words under his breath. This was pathetic. He had a cell phone filled with the names of a number of willing women, women he could call even now, at this hour, to initiate a long-distance booty call. Over the phone, they could engage in some pretty dirty sex talk, and he knew any one of them would follow it up with a visit to the lake by morning. Probably before the sun even came up, there would be a knock at his door. So why was he sitting here with a hard-on as big as the state of Texas?

While he was pondering that question, the light came back on in the bedroom next door. Evidently, Ellie had decided she wasn't ready to go to bed after all. He watched, and then his breathing almost thickened when he saw a slight movement of the curtain, a flutter. Was his imagination getting the best of him?

He slowly stood, deciding he wouldn't torture himself any longer, when the curtain moved again. Actually moved. And then she was there.

At the sight of her he sucked in a deep breath and his already hard body got harder.

She was wearing a pair of shorts and a blouse. He couldn't see all of her shorts but he could see most of her blouse. And it was open. Unbuttoned all the way to her navel. And she wasn't wearing a bra.

He blinked. For a second he couldn't breathe. He refused to do so. He could only watch, stare, all but gape, while making out the fullness of her breasts that he could see from a distance. His lips firmed. Did she have any idea what she was doing?

He dropped back down in the swing with his gaze glued to the window. It was dark over at his place, so Ellie didn't know he was sitting on the porch watching her. Or did she?

He leaned back in his seat. If she was deliberately putting on a show, he fully intended to watch. With a barely functional mind, he took in all he was seeing, and when she slowly eased the blouse from her shoulders, letting it drop nonchalantly to the floor, leaving her bare, he couldn't fight the rampant sensations, the hard-hitting desire that seeing her naked breasts evoked.

Intense heat seared through him, making his already hot body even more enflamed. And as he continued to watch, she leaned over and he could tell she was removing her shorts. After taking them off she held them in her hand, up to her chest, before tossing them aside. And then he could tell she was easing something else off her body and figured it was her panties. Moments later, she held them up on her finger and, as if they were a trophy, she twirled them around in the air on her finger a few times, before tossing them away as well.

The sudden flick of his tongue across his sensitized lips made his breathing almost come out in a growl. He couldn't see much of her below the navel, but just knowing she was completely naked made his pulse increase to heart-attack range. She caressed her stomach the way a lover would, before placing both hands on her naked hips and traveling them lower.... Then she drew the curtains.

He eased out of the swing and putting one foot in front of the other. He moved down the steps, not caring that his bedroom slippers were not meant to be worn outdoors. Nothing mattered except for the woman who'd had the nerve, the audacity and the boldness to tempt him. Excite him to no end. Coax the untamed beast in him to come out.

He stalked through the trees toward her front door. Ellie evidently assumed the show was over. But he was about to let her know, in no uncertain terms, that as far as he was concerned it was just beginning.

Chapter 10

Smiling, Ellie slipped into her nightie. Never in her life had she done anything so brassy and bold. Outlandish. Brazen. And she felt good about it.

There was a chance Uriel hadn't been sitting out on his back porch tonight, and had missed her little show, but that was okay. She had taken the chance, not knowing one way or the other. And she had liked pretending that he was out there, sitting and watching. Getting aroused.

That possibility had made her shamelessly daring. She hadn't intended to do that piece with her panties, but at the last minute she thought she might as well go for the gusto.

She could imagine him staring up at her with that intense look on his face, no smile, just a look of complete concentration, deep, unyielding attentiveness and hot-blooded awareness.

She breathed in deeply. The only problem now was that she was left in a bad way. Being an exhibitionist had made her realize more than ever just how sexually deprived she was. That was why her skin suddenly felt hot to the touch. The juncture of her legs was tingling something awful, and the nipples of her breasts felt tender. She needed to take a cold shower to get rid of all these sensations before she became crazed with lust of the most potent kind.

Deciding a cold shower wasn't such a bad idea, she was about to turn toward the bathroom when she heard a pounding downstairs on her front door. She sucked in a quick breath the same time her pulse began racing. There could only be one person at her door. The same person she had performed her little act for at the window. Evidently, he'd been awake. He had watched. He had interpreted her message.

And he wasn't waiting until tomorrow to let her know that he'd received it.

She stood glued to the spot, not sure what she should do. Maybe if she didn't do anything he would assume she was asleep and go away. Fat chance. She had a feeling she had unleashed the uncontrolled beast in her neighbor, that same wildness she had detected the other day. A controlled Uriel she could handle. An uncontrolled one she wasn't so sure about.

The pounding stopped and she wondered if he'd gone away. Or…had he decided to come into the house anyway? Because her aunt had been getting up in age, both Uriel and his parents knew Aunt Mable kept a spare key taped underneath the cushion of her wicker chair. Would Uriel be so bold as to enter her home uninvited?

Deciding not to wait and find out, she quickly put on her robe and moved toward the stairs. As soon as her feet touched the living room floor the pounding at the door started again.

Nervously, she walked over to the door, having a good idea of the voraciousness of the lust she might have released, not only within herself but within Uriel as well. When she got to the door she leaned on it, could actually feel the fierce pounding of her heart against the heavy wood panel. "Who is it?"

"Uriel."

Hearing his name spoken from such a deep, throaty voice effectively made her heart beat even faster. On tiptoes she looked out the peephole, and although it was dark, she could make out his muscular form in the shadows. At that moment her entire body intensified with a need she hadn't known until tonight that she was capable of feeling.

Her racing pulse didn't abate as she flipped the lock and slowly opened the door. She pulled in a tight breath when they stood facing each other. It was as if he'd walked straight out of his bedroom, wearing nothing more than a dark pair of scandalously sexy shorts and slippers. She held his gaze as intently as he was holding hers, saw that his breathing was just as rapid. Noticed the center of his throat and saw how his pulse rate was beating just as fast as hers.

She was tempted to lick her lips with her tongue, and

then thought better of it upon remembering what the action had sparked within him the last time. Instead she swallowed deeply and said as calmly as she could, "Uri, is there something that you wanted?"

"Yes." He advanced forward, which prompted her to back up when he crossed over the threshold and closed the door behind him. He didn't stop walking until he stood directly in front of her. "There's something I want. And you're it."

Uriel studied the look on Ellie's face. He sharpened his gaze. She knew why he was here, although he could tell she was surprised by his appearance. Did she actually think her little performance at the window wouldn't prompt him to rush right on over and take her up on what she'd been offering?

"I saw you at the window," he said, and when she didn't respond he raised his brow and added, "I assume that was to let me know you've decided on the summer fling. Am I right or wrong?"

She held his gaze and for a second he thought she would claim that he was wrong, and that she had no earthly idea what he was talking about, and that he must have imagined the whole thing. But she didn't. He watched as she gave a little bit of relief to those lips she had pressed so tight and said softly, "No, you're not wrong."

She drew in a deep breath and then added, "But I didn't expect you to come tonight."

He took another step toward her, coming so close the nipples of her breasts pressed against his bare chest through the material of her robe. "You actually thought I would wait?"

"Yes."

His scowl eased into a smile. "Baby, if you thought that, then you don't know men very well. And you most certainly don't know me. But I plan to change that. By the time our fling ends you'll know me better than any other man you've ever been intimate with."

Ellie tightened her lips before she made the mistake of uttering that she hadn't been intimate with many men, and could basically narrow it down to one—which had truly been a waste of her time. But she had a feeling that any time spent with Uriel would not be wasted.

Holding his gaze, she thought about getting to know him intimately. That meant they would be spending a lot of time together between the sheets. But then, wasn't that what she needed to get inspired?

She then thought about how Tamara would handle it if she was in the same dilemma and immediately knew the answer. Tamara was confident with her sexuality and would face up to Grant at every turn. So likewise, Ellie fixed Uriel with a challenging stare and said, "And you'll know me better than any other woman you've ever been intimate with."

She watched as he slowly raised a pair of arrogant brows. Instead of backing down, she slowly raised hers. And then a smile touched the corners of his lips when he said, "We will see, won't we?"

Before she could respond, before she could draw her next breath, he reached for her, pulled her into his arms and sank his mouth down hard on hers.

Resisting never entered her mind, which was just as well, since she was suddenly caged by his masculine strength—a strength that was more comforting than threatening. And when she felt his hard, engorged erection cradle intimately at the juncture of her thighs, she released a satisfied moan and shifted her full concentration into the kiss.

But then, he was making it impossible not to do so, with the way his tongue was taking hold on hers, savoring it like it was something he had missed and was entitled to making up for lost time. Every flick, every lick and every single thrust of his tongue, as it tangled with hers made her moan even deeper. It elicited intense sensations that were uncontrolled and unrestricted. This kiss was even more hot, demanding and overwhelming than the last, and she hung on, determined to keep up, hold her own and stand her ground.

Unexpectedly, he pulled his mouth back and she used that time to suck in a quick breath. When she met his gaze and he smiled, she knew at that moment he hadn't finished with her yet. She saw the heat in his eyes.

"Do you prefer the bed or right here?"

She blinked. He had spoken, and she nearly blushed upon realizing what question he'd asked. The bed would be her logical choice but the other option definitely intrigued her. "Which do you prefer?" she decided to ask him, curious as to what he would say.

His smile widened into a sexy grin and he replied in a low throaty voice, "Doesn't matter. Either way, I plan on making you incapable of speech for a while."

She lifted a brow. His arrogance was showing again. "And what makes you think I won't be able to talk?"

"Because you'll be too busy moaning. That is, when you aren't screaming."

She didn't know what to say to that, figured there was nothing she could say. And when he leaned down and captured her mouth again, she figured some things were better left unsaid. This kiss would have wiped any words right from her mouth, anyway.

He deepened the kiss seconds before sweeping her off her feet and into his arms. He then headed up the stairs, and she knew once they reached the bedroom that she would be getting more than inspired. She would be indulging in passion of the wildest and most exciting kind.

Chapter 11

The trip up the stairs took a little longer than expected, when Uriel stopped midway up, after deciding he just had to taste her mouth again. He wasn't sure why he couldn't wait, all he knew was that he just couldn't.

So, leaning against the rail, he balanced her securely in his arms while taking her mouth with slow deliberation, letting his tongue wrap around hers, mate with it, play with it and entice her to respond. She did. And when she entwined her arms around him and returned the kiss with the same intensity, he deepened the kiss even more.

By the time they reached her bedroom, his entire body was quivering with a need so keen and potent that he had to do everything within his power to hold on to what little control he had. Never had a woman brought him to this.

Never had he felt so connected to a woman in so many ways. Never had he wanted a woman so badly.

The moment he placed her on the bed, he decided wasting time wouldn't get either one of them anywhere, so he reached out and quickly removed her robe and swiftly dispensed with her excuse for a nightgown. It was one of those short nighties with satin spaghetti straps that didn't cover much, not that he was complaining. The cool mint green highlighted her complexion, and the nightie was similar in design to the yellow one she'd been wearing that first night he'd seen her at the window.

When she was stretched out on the bed, reclining on her side facing him, his gaze swept all over her naked body, scanning her from head to toe, absorbing every inch of her. He was fascinated by the perfect details of her body, each and every curve, the flatness of her stomach, the graceful smoothness of her thighs, the allure of her long legs. But what part enticed him the most, what captured his gaze time and time again, was the beauty of her feminine mound. He had seen many in his day, but none that seemed more perfect, more alluring than hers. For him, hers held an unexplainable fascination. She had seen him naked before, but this was his first time he'd seen her without clothes, and he couldn't get enough of looking at her. The more he looked, the harder he got. The more his erection throbbed. And the more it ached to get inside of her.

He could tell that his intense stare was making her nervous, so he backed away from the bed to remove his own clothes, which consisted of nothing more than the pair of nylon gym shorts.

Uriel heard her sharp intake of breath the moment he eased the shorts down his legs. He had come ready. He had come hard. What had she expected, after that number she'd pulled at the window? He had been a goner the moment she'd taken her panties off and twirled them around on her finger.

He slowly moved back to the bed, wanting to touch her all over, taste her everywhere, consume her in a manner that would leave no doubt in her mind that he had left his mark. Easing onto the bed to join her there, she shifted her body to make room and he took his place beside her. They faced each other, gazed into each other's eyes, and he could feel the beat of her heart. He thought she had such an arousing scent, one that was reaching out to him on a primitive level, triggering everything male within him to respond, act and proceed.

He reached out and traced his hand up the side of her body, liking the feel of her soft skin beneath his fingers. He traveled a path and touched her hip, paid special homage to a small birthmark on her upper thigh.

His hand then traveled in slow motion upward, toward her breasts, and when he made an unhurried path around her nipples he heard her groan deep in her throat. Easing her down on her back, he lowered his head and captured a breast in his mouth and began feasting on her. And when she grabbed hold of his head to hold him to her breasts, he responded by sucking harder. He had discovered a long time ago that there was something special about Ellie's taste. It was delectable and was a scrumptious flavor to his tongue. And tonight it was his.

He intended to do whatever it took to make her aware of that fact. He didn't want to encounter any regrets when the sun came up tomorrow. One night would not be enough for him. The next twenty-something days might not be enough for him either. But they would have to do. He would definitely miss their time together, but then all good things eventually came to an end. His parents had shown him that.

"Uri."

He heard her moan and felt her shudder almost uncontrollably beneath his mouth, and knew he had made her come, just from having his mouth on her breasts. He only looked up briefly to see the glow on her face before his mouth began tracing a path down from her breasts toward her belly, and when he took his tongue and drew a wet ring around her navel, her stomach muscles tightened. He liked the feeling beneath his tongue. He liked the sounds she was making. He damn sure liked her.

At that moment, a turbulent sensation washed over him and he knew he had to taste her completely. This wasn't a token hunger that needed to be appeased, this was greed of gigantic proportions, as ravenous as it could get. Her taste, mingled with her just-climaxed scent, was driving him to a state of craziness.

Possession.

And he knew before the night was over he would possess her. That sort of determination seemed odd, out of place for a mere fling, but it was what it was. He would try to make sense of it later. All he knew was that, at this very moment, he had to have Ellie.

With that thought in mind, he pulled away from her

stomach and began easing lower, his attention latched on that part of her that aroused him the most, that small nub at her center that he knew provided its own taste of honey. He was there before she'd realized where he'd gone, and, by the time it registered, he lowered his head and took total and complete custody.

She screamed the moment his tongue entered her, and her scream only fueled his fire, intensified his need to taste her this way. And from her initial reaction, it was quite obvious no man had ever gone down on her before. He found it odd but gratifying—that he would be the first one giving her this experience. A first they would share together.

He immediately tossed the thought from his mind, that when it came to Ellie, they shared a lot of firsts. Like right now. No woman had ever mattered so much, no booty call was worth so much that he'd left his house in the middle of the night like a madman, needing her so desperately. Until Ellie. He had rushed over here to her, barely dressed, and was now lapping up her honeyed nub like his life depended on it. He hadn't been prepared for this.

Uriel quickly pulled his mouth away when he realized just how unprepared he was. He was about to make love to a woman and didn't have a condom. Damn! Another first.

If this was any other woman, he would haul ass in a heartbeat and go back over to his place, take an ice-cold shower, drown in a few beers and go back to bed. But this wasn't any woman. It was a woman he needed now, as he needed air to breathe.

Licking his lips, savoring her honeyed taste, he

slowly eased his body upward and met her gaze. "I rushed over here so fast I didn't bring any condoms with me," he said in a low voice, hating to admit to such a thing that was so unlike him. "Would you happen to have one here?" he asked. And if she did, he hoped like hell it was more than one.

He knew what her answer would be before she opened her mouth to speak, and his entire body became infused with intense disappointment. "No. I haven't been intimately involved with anyone for over four years," she said. "But…"

He blinked. There was a *but*. A semblance of hope sprang to life within him, his erection throbbed even more and he waited for her to continue. When she paused and wouldn't say anything else, he prodded. "But what?"

"I'm on the Pill. I've been on them since high school." She blushed when she added, "To keep me regulated each month."

He could tell she'd gotten embarrassed, sharing such personal information with him. Typically, he preferred his own brand of protection, regardless if the woman claimed she was on the Pill. Unless a man was with a woman 24/7 to watch her take the damn thing, there was no way he could be absolutely sure, and Uriel had better sense than to take any woman's word when it came to birth control. He knew of several guys who had "Pill babies" walking around, that they were paying child support for.

But this wasn't just any woman he was dying to make love to. It was Ellie—and if she said she was on the Pill, he felt confident that she was. So, in essence, she'd just thrown him a life line, one he intended to take. It would be for this one time, he assured himself. He would be well prepared from here on out.

He met her eyes. "I'm a stickler for safe sex, Ellie, and assure you I'm in good physical shape and I get regular checkups, so I know I'm healthy and free of anything." Now that the issue of birth control had been resolved, he felt the need to address another concern.

She nodded. "And I'm healthy as well," she followed his lead by saying. "I get a checkup annually."

Satisfied they had talked about what needed discussing, he leaned up and lowered his mouth to hers, to return her to the state she was in before the interruption. It seemed every bone in his body was on fire at the thought of making love to her in a way he had never done with another woman.

He couldn't help but revel in the sensations that kissing her this way evoked, and she clung to his mouth, accepting all he was doing to hers: feeding greedily, without any restraint. And the thought of making love to her the same way made his erection throb that much more. It was begging for attention, demanding it.

He pulled away from her mouth to raise his body slightly, then to straddle her, to pin her to the huge bed. He reached down to the juncture of her legs and touched her wetness. He had tasted it earlier and knew she was ready. So was he.

He met her gaze when he settled his body in place, so that his erection was right at her entrance. He wanted to be looking into her face, staring into her eyes when he entered her. He wanted to see her expression the moment she felt his unsheathed shaft. Knowing he couldn't hold back any longer, he leaned to her ear, whispered what he intended to do once he got inside her, and when he watched the blush that colored her cheeks, he met her gaze as he slowly entered her.

He kept his eyes locked with hers as he inched slowly, taking his time, savoring each second. She was tight—in a way, too tight to have done this before, and he decided the man before him hadn't known what the hell he was doing. Only when he finally felt her body opening for him, taking him in, letting him forge his way to the hilt, did he release her gaze to lean forward and take her mouth with his.

The kiss—along with the fact that he was buried deep inside of her, and could feel her muscles tighten around him—made him shudder in a way he'd never before done while making love to a woman. He began moving, then withdrawing and thrusting back inside, over and over again. As he did, he threw his head back, thinking this much pleasure was not possible, but every deep stroke into her body only proved that it *was*.

He pulled his mouth from hers and threw his head back to let out one hell of a fierce growl, and his body trembled with a need that had him panting for breath. She screamed then and it echoed off the walls and ricocheted into him, causing him to thrust harder into her, lifting her hips under him, until the force of his release threatened to consume them both.

He greedily took her mouth as the orgasm tore into him, shredding his body into a million pieces and letting him feel each slice cut straight to the core of him, a part he'd always kept well protected. But not now. At this moment, it was open, raw, totally exposed, and he was powerless to fight it.

When the sensations finally ran their course, he felt weakened, totally spent. He slumped down upon her, his muscles unable to move. He'd had orgasms before, but none had left him feeling so sated, so drained. Struggling to ease his weight off her, he pulled her into his arms, and wrestled with what he was feeling, trying to fully understand why making love with Ellie had been so intense, so different and so mind-blowingly perfect.

No, he would think about that later. Much later. For now, all he wanted to do was hold her in his arms while the magnificent sensations rushed through him, leaving him blissfully sated, splendidly drained and gloriously weak.

Ellie sat cross-legged in the bed and stared at Uriel while he slept. He was sleeping so peacefully that, if it hadn't been for the slow movement of his chest denoting he was breathing, she would have wondered if he was still alive.

Over the years, she'd often heard her mother remark about her father's snoring. It was just the opposite with Uriel. If it hadn't been for the warm, hard body that had been next to her, and the solid arms that had held her close all through the night—she would not have known he was in the bed. He had been just that soundless and motionless.

She had never spent the entire night with a man before, and when she awakened during the night it had felt odd.

But knowing the man was Uriel had comforted her, and she had closed her eyes and returned to peaceful slumber.

Now she was wide awake and she couldn't help but sit there and watch him sleep, while remembering all the sensations he had stirred within her. When she had reached the peak of sexual fulfillment, not once but twice during the same lovemaking session, her orgasms had been nothing like she'd ever experienced before. And Uriel had made it happen.

She angled her head as she continued to stare at him. She had never known a more assured man, confident in his abilities. He didn't just talk the talk, he delivered. He had made good on his promise to make her incapable of speaking for a while. She doubted she could speak now. She had very little to say, since she was still in awe of it all. In awe of it and in awe of him, but then it was hard to separate the two.

She glanced over at the clock. It was close to six in the morning, and the sun was peeking up over the mountains. Typically, on most mornings, he would be up, dressed in his gym shorts and in the backyard working out. But today, after a night spent with her, he was still asleep, with no signs of waking up.

Ellie smiled. She would love to think she had worn him out after their night of lovemaking. She would be the first to admit it had been intense.

A small piece of lint off the bedspread had settled in his hair and she wondered if she could remove it without waking him. She leaned over and reached out, and when he suddenly opened his eyes, her hand froze in midair. His dark, intense eyes met hers, and she wondered if he

An Important Message from the Publisher

Dear Reader,

Because you've chosen to read one of our fine novels, I'd like to say "thank you"! And, as a special way to say thank you, I'm offering to send you two more Kimani Romance novels and two surprise gifts – absolutely FREE! These books will keep it real with true-to-life African American characters that turn up the heat and sizzle with passion.

Please enjoy the free books and gifts with our compliments...

Linda Gill

Publisher, Kimani Press

Peel off Seal and Place Inside...

was trying to figure out where he was and why they were in the same bed. She pulled her hand back. "There's a piece of lint in your hair and I was going to get it out," she explained.

He held fast to her gaze and asked in a voice that was raspy from sleep, "Is there?"

"Yes."

His gaze slowly moved from her eyes and shifted upward to her hair. "What do you know? There's a piece of lint in yours as well."

And then he reached out and his hand first went to her hair, before he cupped his hand behind her neck and drew her face down to his, capturing her mouth.

Ellie was so absorbed in the kiss that it took her a while to notice he had shifted positions again and she was now underneath him. After an intense mating session with their tongues, he pulled back and let his gaze run over her. "You put your gown back on," he said in a throaty murmur.

She smiled up at him. "Yes. Aren't you going to go work out this morning?"

He lifted a brow. "And how do you know I work out every morning?"

She shrugged innocently. "It was a lucky guess."

Tilting his head, he studied her for a moment and then said, "I don't think so. Have you been spying on me again?"

She pretended to be taken aback by his accusation and had to keep the laughter out of her voice when she said, "I can't believe you would accuse me of such a thing, Uri."

When he didn't say anything but continued to study

her face, she finally asked, "Well, aren't you going to say something?"

He smiled. "Yes. Do you want to work out with me?"

She couldn't help rolling her eyes. She recalled what he did while working out, and it looked too strenuous for her. Besides, he was too good at it, and there was no way she could keep up. "No, thank you."

"You sure? I can tone things down a bit."

"Don't bother. Besides, I never liked jumping rope anyway."

"And how do you know I jump rope?"

Too late. She'd been caught. She wondered how she was going to get out of this one, then decided to use the same reason she'd used earlier. "I guessed."

"Once again, I don't think so. That means you will be working out with me this morning, and we'll start with my version of push-ups. But first I need to get rid of this." Rising on his knees, and with a quick flick of his wrist, he removed her nightgown.

Then he kissed the surprised gasp from her lips, and by the time he took his mouth away, she felt her bones seem to soften like jelly. "Now," he whispered close to her mouth as he straddled her body, "this is how it's done."

And he proceeded to show her.

Chapter 12

Through exhausted eyes, Uriel watched the delicious sway of Ellie's naked hips as she left the bed to go to the bathroom.

He forced his body to roll over, trying to recall just how many push-ups he'd actually done, so many he'd lost count. The only thing he remembered was that her body had been the mat, and each time he'd lowered down to it, his shaft had been dead center to enter her. The tempo had been quick and rapid, the strokes sure and precise, and when an orgasm tore into her, it tore into him as well; and the final time he came down on her, he locked in to her tightly, as his release exploded inside of her.

He closed his eyes, remembering his vow that last night would be the one and only time he made love to her without a condom. But a condom had been the last thing on his mind every time he'd lowered his body to hers, felt the connection, went inside of her, felt how her inner muscles had tried to clench him before he'd quickly pull out, only to push back in. That had been one hell of a workout, one he doubted he would ever forget.

He opened his eyes when he heard the shower going and had every intention of joining her there. But first he needed to get a second wind. When had any woman made him do that? He glanced over at the clock. It was past ten already. When was the last time he'd stayed in bed this long? Hell, he could barely remember what day it was. All he remembered was how it felt being inside of Ellie, making love to her, releasing a part of himself inside of her.

Uriel closed his eyes again, reliving the moment. He snagged her pillow and buried his face in it, needing to breathe in her scent. He felt at peace, relaxed, sleepy—and although he wanted to join her in the shower, he gave in to sleep.

Ellie stood on her back porch with a cup of coffee in her hand, while gazing out at the lake. It would be another beautiful day because the most beautiful man was upstairs sleeping in her bed. She had expected him to join her in the shower and had been surprised when he hadn't. When she had dried off, and slipped into a pretty pink shorts set, and returned to the bedroom, he was sleeping like a baby.

Going downstairs, she had taken her laptop and—remembering where her aunt's manuscript ended—she picked up from there, to pen her own words, and had been surprised to see just how easily her thoughts had flowed. It had been a scene where Grant and Tamara had met for lunch, and later Grant had invited her to his house. There had been no doubt in either of their minds what would happen when they got there.

Ellie had been surprised just how easily the dialogue had come to her, and she could actually feel the chemistry between them as she typed each word. It was as if she had gotten into their heads. She'd known each time Grant had wanted to reach out and touch Tamara but had fought the urge to do so, still thinking he didn't need or want a woman in his life.

Ellie had not written the lovemaking scene, deciding she wanted her full concentration when she did so, and didn't want to have to worry about Uriel walking in on her and possibly asking questions about what she was doing.

After what they'd shared the night before, she felt inspired, in awe and quietly resigned to the fact that Uriel could stir up passion within her as if it was his right. And those pushups…

Where on earth did he come up with this kind of stuff? He had placed his body in perfect formation over her, his chest flat, arms shoulder level, feet apart and parallel. Even after the first contact with her body, he had kept his body straight, although he had cheated a few times by bringing down his hips for deeper penetration. He thrust inside of her each time he lowered his body, inhaling as he did so, only to exhale when he would raise his body from inside her. He had done two sets of fifty, and she hadn't been able to handle any more, and had tumbled over into an orgasm so strong it nearly drowned them. It seemed her orgasm triggered his, and they both had gotten washed away. She had discovered firsthand just what strong muscles he had.

"Why didn't you wake me?"

She swung around. Uriel was standing in the doorway with a cup of coffee in his hand, and the only stitch of clothing he had on was the gym shorts from last night. Now in the daylight, she could see just how scandalous those shorts looked on him, exposing his muscled thighs and strong legs. She knew how those legs felt cradling hers.

She moved her gaze from the lower part of his body back to his face, and noted the sleepy look in his eyes. Sleepy and sensually hazed over. "I figured you needed your rest," she said, her gaze slipping back to his shorts, specifically the middle, and what was so obvious. Could he be aroused this morning already? But then she'd heard that some men woke up with erections that had nothing to do with sexual desire. However, with the way Uriel was looking at her, she wasn't so sure.

"Have you eaten breakfast already?" he asked, taking a sip of coffee.

She smiled. "No. Are you hungry? I can throw something together in—"

"The reason I asked is because I wanted to treat you to breakfast this morning. I had a good week fishing, and I know how much you like fried fish. At least, you used to like it."

Her smile widened. "I still do."

"Then give me a chance to shower and get things set

up outside. I'm going to use that big fryer Dad stored in one of the closets," he said.

"Wonderful! Is there's something I can do? Anything you need me to bring?"

He didn't say anything as his gaze moved over her, and she could tell by the way he looked at her that he liked her outfit. Figuring she'd be alone at the lake, she'd purchased several shorts sets that were comfortable, feminine and so easy to wear. She'd also figured it'd be hot, although not this kind of hot. The way Uriel stared at her had her blood nearly boiling.

"Uriel?" She tried to get his attention away from her bare legs.

His gaze roamed back up to her face. "Yes?"

"I asked if there was something I could do and if you needed me to bring anything."

He moved away from the doorway and walked toward her. When he came to a stop in front of her, he reached out and brushed a strand of hair from her face. He then lowered his mouth to hers and kissed her in a slow, drugging fashion. The taste of coffee on her tongue mingled with the taste of him. But it wasn't just his taste that she found intoxicating, it was the way he used his tongue. He was a master at making each and every kiss memorable.

He pulled back, met her gaze and said in a husky voice, "I'll let you know what you can do when you get there. And as far as bringing anything, just bring yourself. You will be more than plenty."

He moved away to walk down the steps, and then looked back at her, smiled and said, "I promise to return your coffee cup, but this is the best coffee I've drunk in a long time, Ellie Weston. You're good at everything you do."

She watched him walk away, thinking that if his compliment was meant to butter her up for some reason, it was working.

Ellie decided to prepare something to bring anyway. It was the least she could do, since he was frying the fish. And though it was close to noon, and breakfast had turned into brunch, she would bet any amount of money he would be cooking a pot of grits.

It hadn't taken her long to throw together a container of coleslaw, and while she was at it, she decided a nice desert was in order, so she had baked a batch of peanut-butter cookies, using her aunt's recipe. She even made a pitcher of lemonade, Mable Weston's own blend.

While the cookies were baking, she sat at the kitchen table with her laptop. Although she couldn't see him from where she sat, Ellie could hear the commotion Uriel was making as he set up the deep fryer outside. The last time she recalled it had been used was for Uriel's eighteenth birthday party.

His birthday was in September, but his parents had decided to celebrate a month early, since he would be leaving home and going off to college at the end of August—and it would have been the ideal time for his five godbrothers to attend. That had been the last time she had seen all six of them together. As she made her way over to Uriel's, she thought it was wonderful that the men had stayed in contact all these years.

"I was wondering when you would get here," Uriel said, smiling at her when she appeared through the trees. He hurried over to take some of the items from her hands. He was wearing a pair of denim cutoffs and a T-shirt.

"What's all this?" he asked. "I thought I told you that you didn't have to bring anything."

She returned his smile. "I know, but I couldn't resist. There's nothing like coleslaw to go along with fish and grits. And I couldn't resist baking some of those peanut-butter cookies you love so much."

His eyes lit up. "You have your aunt's recipe?"

She laughed. "Of course. Aunt Mable left me everything." She refrained from saying: including her unfinished manuscript. "I've even made a pitcher of lemonade that I need to go back to get."

She glanced around and saw he'd already placed several pieces of fish in the fryer. She knew they had been coated with his father's fried fish batter recipe, and the aroma of mouth-watering fried fish was circulating through the air. "It seems like you have everything under control," she said, smiling over at him.

He grinned. "Did you doubt for one moment that I would?"

"No, not really. If it's okay, I'll go inside and put the slaw in the refrigerator."

"No problem, go ahead."

"Thanks."

"And while you're in there, how about grabbing me that hush puppy batter I have in the fridge."

"Okay."

The moment Ellie opened the back door and went

inside Uriel's home, memories assailed her and she glanced around the kitchen. Everything basically looked the same, and she was surprised he hadn't made any changes. Maybe that had been deliberate, and he wanted to remember earlier times when his parents had been happy together, or so he'd assumed. She wondered if he knew the reason behind his parents' failed marriage of thirty-plus years, and if it had a bearing on how he viewed relationships. She hoped not. But then, she would be the first to admit that she believed in a strong marriage for herself, because her parents had one. If she found out different, would she think otherwise? She didn't think so, but one could never be absolutely sure how they would react in certain situations.

After placing the slaw in his refrigerator she remembered he had asked her to bring back the hush puppy batter, so she grabbed the foil-wrapped container. Moments later she was headed back outdoors, but stopped when she got to the screen door, and glanced out. She couldn't stop the grin that touched her lips. Standing in front of the fryer with tongs in his hand, Uriel looked relaxed, as if he was actually enjoying what he was doing.

Just as he'd enjoyed what he'd been doing last night as well. At least he had given her the impression that he had enjoyed himself. She knew that *she* had. He was an experienced man in the bedroom, and there was so much he could teach her, so many ways to inspire her. But a part of her knew finishing the manuscript was only a small part of her wanting to be with Uriel. She would be fooling herself if she convinced herself otherwise. She truly wanted to be with him—to spend whatever time she could with him was a dream come true for her, and she intended to be satisfied with that.

He must have felt her gaze on him, because at that moment he looked over her way and smiled. "Are you standing there drooling over me or the fish?" he asked, taking a few pieces out of the fryer. She all but licked her lips when she saw they were a golden brown.

"The fish," she said smiling, as she opened the screen door and walked out on the porch. "Why on earth would I be drooling over you? And here's the hush puppy batter."

"Thanks, just set it on that table. The first batch is out, hot and ready to eat, just as soon as I get a few hush puppies going. I hope you're hungry."

"Starving. I'm going to get the lemonade. Is there something I can do or get for you before I leave?"

"Yes, there is something. Come here for a second."

She actually thought he was going to ask her to watch the fish while he took a bathroom break, and when she reached out for the frying tongs, he reached out for her. Before she had a chance to react, he bent his head and took her mouth.

Desire as hot as the fryer oil raced through her body with his kiss. When he pulled back, her senses felt totally wrecked. She could only stand there in a daze and look at him.

He smiled. "You can go get the lemonade now."

His words made her blink, and she felt a little embarrassed that she'd been standing there, starting at him like a ninny. "Yes, of course."

As she made her way along the path toward her house, she could only fight the fires that were beginning to rage out of control inside her.

And she knew at that moment that a summer fling with Uriel might be more than she could handle, if day one was anything to go by.

Chapter 13

Uriel kept his gaze glued to Ellie until she was no longer in sight. He actually felt the area behind his zipper throb. Okay, so maybe he should have a little more control; but seeing a small waist, flat tummy, curvy hips and a nice tight backside in a pair of denim shorts could do it to him. Nothing could ignite a man's testosterone quicker than a sexy female body, and memories of how it felt being inside that particular body was enough to raise anything. Especially an erection.

He had gotten the last of the fish out of the fryer and had tossed in the hush puppies when his cell phone went off. After wiping his hand on a paper towel, he pulled the phone from his back pocket. "Yes?"

"Start the fish frying, we're on our way."

Uriel frowned upon recognizing Xavier's voice. "I

thought you had other plans, X, and who are we?" Now that he and Ellie had decided on a summer fling, the last thing he wanted was company. He had a specific agenda already laid out in his head, and from the look and feel of things last night, they were off to a very good start. He'd known his godbrothers would visit him sooner or later, but a part of him wished it was later.

"My plans for the weekend got canceled, and we are me, Virgil, Winston, and York. They showed up this morning to visit your Dad, only to discover he's out of the country."

Anthony Lassiter and his friends had forged a tight bond in college and had passed that bond onto their first sons. The elder men had made themselves a part of their godsons' lives. They were men who had set good examples and were deeply admired and respected. Men who in some way, some form or fashion, had always been there for their godsons. Therefore, it wasn't unusual for the younger men to show up, individually or collectively, to check on one of their godfathers. Especially if their health and well-being was an issue. And although Uriel could thankfully say his father's state of mind had improved a lot, his well-being continued to be a concern. A broken heart was worse than a hard kick in the ass. It was a torment that didn't seem to go away. It was the kind of misery that loved company, and it was something Uriel definitely didn't want for himself.

"Dad flew to Rome on business, and he plans to check on Zion while he's there," Uriel said, wondering how long his godbrothers would be staying, once they got to the lake. Uriel had all intentions of sharing Ellie's bed again tonight, and their arrival would throw a monkey wrench into his plans.

"Where are you guys now?" he decided to ask.

"Less than thirty minutes away. We'll be there before you know it. Do you need us to stop and get anything? Need more beer?" Xavier was asking.

"No, I got plenty," Uriel responded. "You might want to pick up some wine coolers, though. You know how much Winston likes them."

"Okay, we can do that. We'll see you soon."

He heard the sound of Ellie returning when he placed his cell phone back in his pocket. He turned toward her when she stepped into the clearing from among the trees, carrying a pitcher of ice-cold lemonade. He thought it would be best to let her know his godbrothers were coming.

"We're going to need additional food, so I'm going to cook more fish," he said, taking the hush puppies out of the fryer.

"Why?" she asked, with a bemused expression on her face.

"Xavier just called. He, Winston, York and Virgil are headed this way. They'll be here in a half hour or so."

He watched as a smile touched Ellie's face. "It will be nice to see them again." Without hesitating, she added, "I'll put this pitcher of lemonade in your refrigerator, and then I'll go back home to make some more slaw. I baked enough cookies the first time around," she said.

"Okay."

He watched as she walked up the steps to his porch and then went inside, thinking how good she looked in those cutoff shorts that showed a lot of shapely thigh, and he knew, if he noticed it, his godbrothers would notice as well. They were all hot-blooded bachelors.

When Ellie came out of the house, he said, "I prefer being the only man to see you in those sexy-looking shorts while we're involved, Ellie."

He could tell from her expression that his statement surprised her, had caught her off guard. She lifted her chin, probably to put him in his place about thinking he could dictate what she wore, but after their gazes held for a while, she lowered it. He could actually feel heat, desire and longing stroke across his skin, and after their gazes locked for several moments, he could tell that her entire body began to relax. They were in an intimate relationship, and he felt territorial. He could tell that at some point during the last few moments she had decided that she would accept what he'd said as his due for now. "That's fine," she finally said in a yielding tone, before turning to head back over to her place.

No, it wasn't fine, he thought, placing more fish into the batter. He'd never been concerned with the outfit worn by any woman he was involved with, or who might be seeing her in it, no matter how sexy the outfit might have looked. He'd never had a jealous bone in his body. So why was he growing one now?

Uriel turned and looked out at the lake. He needed to think over a few things. Namely, why, for the first time in his life, he was acting like a jealous man.

Ellie looked at her outfit in the mirror. She had changed out of her shorts and top set, and was wearing a pale-yellow, crinkled chiffon blouse and a printed flowing skirt with bright yellow daisies. This was another new outfit she had purchased.

She thought about Uriel's request that she change outfits. She would have done so anyway, just because she'd known her shorts would be considered a little too much…or in this case, a little too little, to go parading around wearing, especially among a group of men. To hear Uriel make the suggestion, though, like she hadn't had the sense to know that, at first had gotten her ire up. But, when she had met his gaze, she had seen the possessiveness in the dark depths of his eyes. They had made love. Twice. Had spent the night in each other's arms. Uriel was a man, and once in awhile they got foolish thoughts about certain things. As far as she was concerned, this was one of those times. She figured sooner or later he would figure that out on his own, without any prodding from her. But for now, although what they were sharing was nothing more than a summer fling, if he wanted to be territorial and protective, she'd let him have his way.

When she made it back down to the kitchen, she heard the sound of several car doors slamming. She glanced out the living-room window in time to see four men walking up the steps to Uriel's front door.

She studied the men's faces, and although she hadn't seen them since the summer of their last year of high school, she still recognized them. Like Uriel, they were in their early thirties. All were very good-looking—*handsome* would be an even better word to describe them—and, according to Uriel, like him, they were still single.

Going into the kitchen and grabbing the cole slaw out of the refrigerator, she headed out the door.

Uriel couldn't help but smile as he gazed at the four men. Although they might be screwing up his plans with Ellie, he was still glad to see them. They were close—always had been and always would be. Of the six of them, he and Xavier were the only two who didn't have other siblings. But the one thing they all had in common was that they were the first-born sons of their fathers.

"Okay, U, where's the food?" Winston Coltrane asked, looking around and sniffing the air. Everyone knew how much Winston loved to eat, especially when it came to fried fish from Cavanaugh Lake.

"In the kitchen. And there's plenty, W, so don't plan on eating any off Y's plate," Uriel said laughing. Since being kids, they'd shorten each other's names with just the first letter.

At that moment there was a knock at the door. York, a former officer for the NYPD, who now owned his own security firm, glanced over to Uriel. "You're expecting someone, U?"

Uriel nodded. York was always on the alert for any type of action. "Yes, I'm expecting someone," he said, crossing the room to the front door. He understood why Ellie would come to the front door instead of the back door. She wasn't sure how he wanted to define their relationship to his godbrothers, and would follow his lead. He appreciated that, because he wasn't sure how he intended to define it—which was odd, because he'd never had this problem before with other women.

He opened the door and his mouth nearly fell open. She had changed clothes, but if she thought what she was wearing would garner less attention, she was sadly mistaken. This was the first time he recalled ever seeing her in anything other than shorts, and the transformation was astounding. The color yellow made her glow in a sensuous sort of way. And the smile she wore jolted his insides.

"I'm back with the cole slaw," she said in a quiet tone, and the texture of her words seemed to flow over his skin. Instead of answering or taking the huge bowl out of her hands, he just stood there staring at her. She'd done something different to her hair. It was all fluffed up around her face, as though she'd put a curling iron to it. And he could also tell she'd put on some makeup. Not a whole lot, but just enough to enhance her full cheeks and eyes. Then there was the lip gloss she'd smoothed on her lips, which made them even more sultry-looking. He felt tempted to lean closer and taste them.

"Hey, who's at the door, U?"

Uriel rolled his eyes. It was Y asking again. Instead of answering, he took the bowl out of Ellie's hands and whispered for her ears only, "Yellow is my favorite color on you."

When her smile brightened even more, he said, "Come on in." He took a step back and hoped he would be able to deal with his godbrothers when they saw her again.

When Uriel stepped out of the way, Ellie walked over the threshold and four pair of eyes stared straight at her. From the curious expressions on their faces, she knew immediately they didn't remember her, which was understandable, since she'd only been twelve years old when she'd last seen them.

Smiling, she said, "Hi guys. It's good seeing you again."

Their gazes sharpened, it seemed all at the same time. One man's eyes narrowed more than the others, and she recalled who he was: York Ellis. And he was the one who finally lifted a brow of disbelief when he said, "L?"

The others followed with that same astonished disbelief in their voices. She could only chuckle, and said, "Yes, it's me."

"Damn."

That had come from Virgil Bougard, and it made her laugh. He still could curse.

Over the summers, when they had visited with Uriel at the lake, they had called each other by the first letter of their names, and had told her if she wanted to hang around them and fish—which she did—she had to do likewise. However, they'd said the name "E" didn't do her justice, so she became "L".

"It's been a while," Xavier Kane said, smiling. "The last time we saw you, you were only a kid. How old are you now?"

"She's twenty-six," Uriel said, coming to stand beside her.

"Twenty-six…." Winston Coltrane said, as if rolling the age around on his tongue, while his gaze moved all over her from head to toe.

"Yes, she's twenty-six, but don't even think it," Uriel said in a steely voice.

Winston met his gaze and Ellie glanced over at Uriel

as well, thinking he was sounding territorial again. She quickly decided to downplay his actions by diverting Winston, "And how have you been doing, Winston? Do you still have problems with allergies?"

Winston returned his gaze to her and smiled. "No. I must have outgrown them, since I don't have those problems anymore."

But he did have a problem with being a womanizer, Ellie thought, although she doubted he saw it as a problem. It was something she had picked up on from the way he'd been looking at her, which had all but caused Uriel to growl.

"Well, I brought over some cole slaw and also baked some cookies. I'll help Uriel get things set up in the kitchen. It's good seeing all of you again."

"Same here," they said, almost simultaneously.

She was halfway out of the living room when she overheard Winston whisper to Uriel, "Is that the way it is, U?"

And Uriel's response was firm. "Yes, that is the way it is."

Uriel glanced around at his godbrothers, satisfied they had a clear understanding that Ellie was off-limits, which was a good thing. Now he could relax, since it seemed they were all treating her like the kid sister, as they always had. Everyone was enjoying her company, and she was enjoying theirs, as well.

And although he and Ellie had only hours ago agreed to engage in a summer fling—it was easy to see they were a couple. When she found a place to sit at the table to eat, it seemed natural for him to sit down beside her.

And, more than once, he had found himself just staring at her, listening to her and his godbrothers converse. That was good because he liked looking at her.

There was something about her blouse, how soft it looked next to her skin, that made him want to reach out and touch it, touch her, rub his hand across her flesh, caress it, taste it. He remembered the taste of her and longed to have her again.

"What's Donovan up to these days?" York asked, pulling Uriel's attention momentarily from Ellie.

"Donovan is doing fine. He's at the races this weekend," Uriel responded. "He called a few days ago to let me know he's engaged."

Shock, total and complete, covered the faces of all the men at the table. "Are you saying that Donovan Steele met some woman who he wants to marry?" York asked, as if he refused to believe such a thing was possible.

"Yes, and it shocked the hell out of me, too. But I met her. She's nice, and a looker," Uriel said. He then glanced over at Xavier. "You've met her, too, right, X?"

Xavier stopped eating long enough to nod. A smile touched his face. "Yes, I met her. She is nice. But I have to admit, the night I met her I was more interested in getting to know her friend."

"Who's Donovan?" Ellie interrupted the conversation to ask.

Uriel glanced over at her and said, "Donovan Steele is a good friend of mine from college, and he and I are in several business ventures together. His company, the Steele Corporation, sponsors a car racing team at NASCAR."

She nodded. "Oh. And why is it so strange for him to become engaged?"

Uriel smiled. "Because he was a devout bachelor. The last person anyone would have thought to consider marrying."

Uriel decided not to add that there was no reason for Donovan to ever consider marrying, because he'd had his pick of affairs. In fact, he had lived for them. Why would a sane man give that up? And Donovan was a sane man. The thought of any woman messing with a man's mind to the point where he'd give up his bachelorhood was simply not good.

He glanced over and saw that Ellie had resumed eating her food. Uriel was about to go back to eating his as well, when he happened to glance across the table and saw his godbrothers all staring at him.

He stared back and read the message in their eyes. Like him, they were all bachelors on demand, which meant that they knew whatever was going on between him and Ellie was short-term. He could tell they weren't particularly overjoyed at the thought of that. Although they understood and supported his desire to remain single, and that it meant he would sow wild oats from time to time, he knew they weren't crazy that the recipient of those oats was Ellie.

Hell, he refused to let them try to make him feel guilty about anything. As he'd told them, Ellie was no longer the twelve-year-old they remembered. She was twenty-six, and old enough to make her own decisions about what she wanted to do.

"How long do you all plan to stay?" he decided to ask them.

It was York who responded. "Probably until tomorrow. Why?"

He smiled, but the smile didn't quite reach his eyes, or his lips for that matter, when he said, "No particular reason. Just asking."

They knew there *was* a particular reason, just like he did. At the silence, Ellie, who'd been concentrating on picking bones out of her fish, glanced up. She looked first at Uriel and smiled, before glancing over at Virgil, Winston, Xavier and York. She smiled at them, too, and they smiled back. When she resumed what she was doing, they dropped the smiles off their faces and glared back at Uriel.

He shrugged and continued eating, refusing to let their attitudes bother him. Moments later, Ellie interrupted the quietness that had once again descended around the table to ask, "Where's Zion?"

It was Xavier who spoke. "Z has been living in Rome for a couple of years now. You do know that he's that well-known jeweler, Zion, right?"

Ellie nodded. "Yes, I know," she said, smiling proudly. "I've seen a few of his pieces, and they're simply beautiful. When the president presented the first lady with a Zion bracelet for her birthday, I knew it was just a matter of time before everyone discovered what gorgeous jewelry he designs," she said.

Uriel took a sip of his lemonade. For some reason, he could picture her wearing her own Zion bracelet, one specifically designed just for her. He could also envision a Zion ring on her finger. He blinked, and then frowned, when he realized just where his thoughts were about to go, and he outright refused to let them go there.

He gave himself a quick mental shake, and for the rest of the meal he ate in silence, deciding it would be safer to just listen to the conversation and not add anything to it…and to keep all those foolish thoughts out of his head.

"It was so nice seeing your godbrothers again, and spending time with them, Uriel. They're as nice as I remembered," Ellie said, as Uriel walked her home later that evening. He didn't have to bother, but he'd insisted because it had gotten dark.

After they'd eaten dinner and dessert, everyone had sat around talking about basically everything. The guys had brought her up-to-date on what had been going on with them and about the different businesses they owned. When she'd teased them about them getting married one day, all four of Uriel's friends rebuffed the very thought of doing anything like that.

She wondered what they had against settling down with the right person, and was tempted to ask Uriel, but figured it was none of her business. Still, she couldn't stop wondering if Uriel felt the same way they did. Was he as dead-set against the idea of marriage as they were? Was that the reason he had stipulated they would share nothing more than a short-term affair?

"I won't be coming over tonight, Ellie."

She glanced up at him, saw the tenseness in his jaw, the firmness of his lips, and knew he didn't like the idea of not spending the night with her. In a way, she felt good that he was regretting it. "That's okay, I understand. It wouldn't look right for you to leave your company."

He stopped walking and she did, too. "Do you understand that I enjoyed being with you this morning, making love to you, cherishing your body? I also enjoyed the time we spent together today, even if we weren't alone."

She couldn't help but smile. "Thanks, Uriel. I enjoyed being with you, too." And although she wanted to convince herself it was just for inspiration to finish her aunt's book, she knew that wasn't the reason.

When they reached her porch, instead of walking her up the steps to where they would be standing underneath a bright light—giving his houseguests something to see, he touched her arm and walked her over to the huge oak tree, whose branches not only provided shade but also privacy.

When Ellie stood facing him, Uriel studied her features for a second and said, "You look very pretty today, Ellie."

And she had. He had stared at her a lot today, on the pretense of watching out for her. But he knew that wasn't the case. Not one of his godbrothers, even Winston, would have crossed the line once he had established it. And he *had* established it with Winston's question. Now they pretty much knew something was going on between him and Ellie, but they probably weren't sure just to what extent.

As far as Uriel was concerned, they didn't have to know. They'd never kept up with any of his conquests before. Something cut deep within Uriel with the word conquest. For some reason, he didn't like thinking of Ellie that way.

"Uriel."

He blinked. Her saying his name reined in his attention. He had been staring at her, but his mind had been flooded with other thoughts. Thoughts of her, but also of his godbrothers. Now he wanted his full concentration on Ellie.

Reaching out, he took her chin in his hand, finally allowing himself to taste the lips he'd been looking at all day, and yearned to kiss. He slowly ran his finger across her lips, liking how soft they felt to his touch, all the while his gaze held hers. "I'm going to miss you tonight," he said in a low voice, one that had deepened to a pitch he hadn't known existed for him.

Although her eyes had begun to darken with the same desire he felt, she managed a small smile and said, "I can always stand at the window and give you something to think about—to remember."

A smile touched his lips, followed by a deep frown. "Don't even think about it. I might not be the only one watching," he said, knowing a couple of his godbrothers had a tendency to get up through the night. "That sort of performance is strictly for me."

While we are together in this summer fling, he thought, but didn't say. When things ended between them, would she be sending out intimate messages to other men? He fought back the knot that began forming in his stomach at the mere thought of that happening. He breathed in deeply, deciding what she did after the summer was her business. He would return to Charlotte and resume his life as it had always been. He would bury himself in work and escalate his sex life up a notch.

But now he just wanted to concentrate on Ellie. His fingers moved from her lips, and he then used his hands to frame her face, capture it gently and tilt it up slightly, at the same time that he lowered his head. The last thought on his mind, before their lips touched, was that he needed this just as he needed to breathe. When she uttered a delicious sigh, it gave his tongue the opening it needed to enter her mouth and taste her delectable warmth. The moment he did so, he heard a groan emit from deep within his throat.

He'd figured he would go easy on her mouth, savor it. A hunger, a need, an absolute greed, made it impossible to do that. Instead, his tongue swept all over her mouth, intensifying the heat, stoking the fire and making him want to stand there and kiss her forever.

Forever? He was suddenly stunned at the thought of that word with regard to any woman. Why would he want to kiss the same woman forever, when there were others out there whose mouths probably tasted just as good? But as he deepened the kiss, a part of him knew it would be hard finding one. At the moment, he was satisfied with this mouth. Ellie's mouth. So utterly satisfied that he could feel blood rushing through his veins, and his erection starting to throb. And he knew at that moment, more than just heat was flowing between them. Desire, as compact as it could get, was invading their senses, and it wouldn't take much to pull her down on a bed of grass and make love to her here. Right now. Forever.

The fear of that one word, of even thinking it again,

had him pulling back, stepping away. "I need to go," he said, pulling in a deep breath. "Go on inside, Ellie."

She looked at him, seemed to study his features a moment, before turning and walking up the steps. It was only after she was inside and the door was closed that he leaned back against the oak tree to release the breath he'd been holding. Spending time at his own place, instead of over here, was probably the best thing. He was beginning to act stupidly and think foolishly, and he couldn't allow that to happen. He was a Bachelor in Demand, the last of what seemed to be a dying breed, and he intended to remain that way for life. And no woman, not even someone like Ellie, would make him forget it.

Unable to sleep, Ellie sat in her darkened bedroom and gazed out the window at the house next door. It seemed every room in Uriel's house was lit, which meant everyone was still up and moving around. She knew it had to be close to three in the morning.

When she'd returned home, after taking a shower and changing into a nightgown, she had pulled out her laptop and had typed several scenes, amazing herself at how easily her thoughts had flowed. She had even glanced over her shoulder a few times to make sure her aunt wasn't there somewhere, guiding her fingers across the keyboard, generating the thoughts going through her mind that she was transferring into her laptop. It seemed so easy to continue to read Grant's mind, to see the hard stone around his heart slowly being chipped away. She would admit that he was a complicated man, but he was a man worth loving, and she was glad Tamara knew that.

As before, Ellie wasn't ready to write any lovemaking scenes just yet, although she'd already been inspired by Uriel. Her aunt had done more than connect two bodies in bed, she had created a masterpiece with words enticing the reader to feel, to discover, from the very first kiss. She couldn't attempt to even try to follow in her aunt's footsteps until she felt the time was right.

Sighing deeply, Ellie moved away from the window and crawled back into bed. Funny how after one night, her bed seemed so lonely without Uriel in it. But his masculine scent was embedded in the sheets and the pillow where he had placed his head. She pulled it to her, breathed in deeply, and for the moment she was content.

Chapter 14

"And what if we told you we've decided to stay with you another week, U?" Xavier asked, grinning as Uriel walked them out to their car.

Uriel frowned. "Then I would tell the four of you to check into a hotel," he said bluntly.

Winston glanced through the trees at the house next door. He then rubbed his chin thoughtfully. "Hmm, if you won't put us up for awhile, maybe L will," he said smiling.

Uriel didn't crack a smile. Instead, he crossed his arms over his chest and said, "Go ahead, W, and try me. I haven't kicked your ass in a long time."

"Sounds like somebody won't be a bachelor on demand pretty soon," York said, chuckling.

Uriel's frown deepened. "If so, I don't know who that will be, because I'm staying put. There's nothing different with what's going on with me and Ellie than with any other woman I've dated. This is no big deal, so why are you making it one?"

Virgil shook his head. "No, U, you're making it one, and what's so sad is that you haven't realized it yet. You didn't pick any woman to mess around with, you picked L. Even if we thought it was okay, and really not any of our business—which I have to admit it's not—you still have Ms. Mable to deal with."

Uriel lifted a brow. "Ms. Mable?"

Virgil nodded.

Uriel rolled his eyes. "The woman died, or have you forgotten?"

"No, I haven't forgotten. And the way I figure, she's probably rolling over in her grave, thinking about how you plan to treat her niece. Her favorite niece. Her only niece. Her—"

"If you're trying to make me feel guilty, V, it won't work," Uriel broke into Virgil's spiel to say.

Virgil shook his head. "In that case, we're out of here. We'll see you in Aspen in a few months, right?"

"I'll be there."

"And let L know we'll be seeing her again soon," York added. At the dark, threatening look that suddenly flashed in Uriel's eyes, York couldn't help but laugh. "Damn, man, you got it bad."

The four men then got inside their car and drove away.

Moments later, Uriel was still standing in the same spot. The car was no longer in sight. Even when the last of the dust generated from the car on the dirt road was settling back down to earth, he remained in place.

He still hadn't cracked a smile, because basically, his godbrothers were wrong. They were assuming things they shouldn't. Things about his and Ellie's relationship that weren't there. He and his godbrothers were close, but they couldn't read his mind. But still, they knew his situation better than anyone. They knew that, although he'd pretended nonchalance, his parents' divorce had not only thrown him for a loop but had made him look at things differently.

Ellie was a nice girl, and he hoped she would meet someone who would give her all the things in life she deserved. That man was not him, and would never be. All there was between them was a casual relationship. Ellie knew the score. He wanted her, and yes, it was all about sex and nothing more, but she was a grown woman, not a kid. She could handle it. It had taken almost three days for her to make up her mind, which meant she had thought long and hard about it. That night she had appeared at the window undressed, and had waved her panties in the air, it had been an acceptance by her of that decision. Her acknowledgment of what was and what wasn't. No love, just sex.

He glanced at his watch. He had been standing at the kitchen window this morning when he'd seen Ellie back her car out of the garage. She had gotten out of the car to go back inside the house to get something, and he'd seen she was dressed for church, evidently to attend early morning service. She'd been the epitome of a classy lady, from the dressy, wide-brimmed red hat she'd worn, to her red patent leather high-heel shoes. Her dress was black, with a huge, front-draped red sash around her small waist.

He had been tempted to go out on the porch and at least say good morning, and to tell her how nice she looked. Hell, nice wasn't a strong enough word. She had looked absolutely gorgeous. But he hadn't gone to the porch, for fear he would have eventually crossed his yard to hers and end up kissing her like a man with no control. Just as he was feeling now.

That was the main reason he knew he should get inside the house, trade his jeans for a pair of shorts, get a beer out the fridge and chill a while. Sit on his back porch and appreciate what a beautiful day it was, and be grateful, in spite of what was going on with his parents, that life was good. His business interests appeared to be productive and worthy of every cent he'd invested.

Going back inside and getting that beer sounded like a good plan. Then why was he still standing in the same spot, looking over his right shoulder at the house next door? Why was there an intense longing beginning to build in the pit of his stomach? And why was he turning, placing one foot in front of the other and moving in the direction of where he knew Ellie to be?

And now that he'd passed through the trees and was in the clearing, why was he making his heart rate increase even more by jogging the rest of the way? And why, the closer he got, could he detect her scent, like it was in the very air he was breathing, fueling his heat and intensifying his hunger?

The next thing he knew, he was standing at her back door, leaning against the frame, nearly out of breath—which was unheard of for a man who had a constant workout regime. What he was feeling was anxiousness, not exhaustion. Pulling in a deep breath, he knocked on the door.

She must have been in the kitchen already, because he immediately heard the sound of her voice when she called out, "Just a minute."

While pulling in another deep breath, he heard her footsteps moving across the tile floor. And when she slowly slid the door open and he saw her, looked into her face before moving his gaze to scan over her, to take in yet another sexy short set, he actually couldn't say anything. He just stood there and feasted his eyes on her, feeling a need that for her just couldn't be normal.

His gaze returned to her face and met her eyes. He didn't say anything, but neither did she. However, he figured she'd seen the appreciative male look in his eyes when he'd checked out her outfit. And he was also certain she could see the hunger that was there now. Hunger for something he'd gotten a chance to sample yesterday and was eager to do so again. He'd never considered himself a horny bastard until now.

He could blame his state on a lot of things: he could blame it on the air that for some reason seemed thick with her scent; or the fact that last night he'd hung around four guys who had nothing better to do than share exaggerated tales of their bedroom escapades while drinking beer and eating pretzels. At least three of them had. Come to think of it, Xavier hadn't said a word, which suddenly made Uriel wonder why.

"Uriel?"

He blinked at the sound of Ellie saying his name, but

didn't respond. He couldn't. He just continued to look at her and then, finally, he said, "They're gone."

She nodded. "I know. I was standing at the sink washing dishes, and saw them leave."

That meant she probably saw him standing a while after they'd left, trying to make up his mind what he should do. She probably even saw him jog over to her house like a madman, which was probably why she hadn't asked who was at the door when he'd knocked. She had known.

Suddenly, something passed through his nostrils and he picked up another scent other than hers. Spaghetti sauce. He lifted a brow. "You cooked?"

A smile touched her lips. "A girl's got to eat. I have plenty left, if you want some."

Heat suffused his body. He was hungry, but it wasn't the thought of consuming spaghetti that had certain parts of him throbbing. He wanted her. He wanted to get inside of her. The spaghetti could wait. "May I come in?" he tried asking softly, but the words came out sounding rather husky, even to his own ears.

Instead of answering, she took a step back and he followed, hoping by the time he stepped over the threshold the flames that were raging wildly through his veins would have suddenly cooled. That wasn't the case. The moment he closed the door behind him and, with a flick of his wrist, put the lock in place, he reached out and grabbed her by the waist to bring her closer to him. He wanted her to feel his hardness and to know what wanting her was doing to him. As much as he liked seeing a pair of sexy-looking shorts on her, he suddenly wanted them off her. But first he wanted to kiss her. He *had* to kiss her.

He lowered his head and took her mouth with a kiss that was meant to temporarily satisfy the flames that refused to cool, intended to slow down the fast beating of his pulse. Instead, it ignited a bigger blaze, one that amounted to a bonfire by the time he took hold of her tongue, mingled it with his and started sucking on it. And his pulse, the one he wanted to slow down, actually picked up speed, which then triggered a blood rush through his veins, making his nerve endings feel as if they would explode.

He wasn't sure at what point something within him snapped, pushed him over the edge, made him crazy with lust, desperate for her. But it happened and he couldn't stop it. His rational mind became irrational. His senses lost all commonality. The need to strip out of his clothes and to get her out of hers was as urgent as anything he'd ever endured.

He groaned deep within the pit of his stomach when he forced his mouth from hers. His hands went immediately to his shirt, nearly tore it from his body, sent buttons flying everywhere. He glanced over at her when his hands went to the snap on his jeans. She was leaning against the counter, drawing in deep breaths as she tried to breathe.

She was staring at him through glazed eyes, watching as he kicked off his sandals. Then, in one smooth sweep, he pulled down his jeans and kicked them aside. Before she could react to seeing him standing stark naked in the middle of her kitchen, he had reached out for her and was pulling her top over her head.

Before removing her bra, he leaned down and kissed her again, and while his mouth was busy on hers, his hands were inching downward, inside her shorts, just enough to slip past her panties and go straight for the center, finding her hot, wet and pulsating to his touch.

He actually let out a low growl as he lifted his head, ending the kiss, and bringing his hands upward to take off her bra. Within seconds, his mouth was there on her breasts, feasting greedily on her nipples like a starved maniac.

"Uriel."

The sound of her moaning his name in a shuddered breath alerted him she was close, too close. She was about to come, but he intended to be inside her when she did. Backing her up against the refrigerator, he quickly pulled down her shorts and panties and then kicked them aside, lifted her up and wrapped her legs around his waist. He pinned her between him and the fridge, and entered her with one powerful thrust.

He felt her inner muscles around him begin to throb, start clenching him, and he drew back out and pushed back in, over and over again. They were skin-to-skin, flesh-to-flesh. Her legs were wrapped tightly around his back, and when she screamed out his name, the sound triggered an explosion within him that ripped everything out of him, blasted him off to another hemisphere, made him call her name at the top of his voice, and made him give her all that he had, and then some.

Moments later, he slumped against her, his body still intimately connected to hers. He pulled back, but did not pull out, and looked at her. Her eyes were closed, her face damp with perspiration, her hair falling in her face, and her lips swollen, begging to be kissed.

He leaned and kissed them, still needing to draw this out for as long as he could take it, needing to be connected to her in every way, as long as he desired. And he desired it with every ounce of the strength he'd lost making love to her.

And then, when he couldn't play it out any longer, he swept her into his arms, not caring at the moment that their clothes were thrown carelessly all over her kitchen. He moved through her living room and walked up the stairs, and when they got to her bedroom they tumbled onto her bed and Uriel pulled her into his arms. He spooned her naked body to his, their legs entwined and his hands protectively placed on her stomach. "Rest," he whispered in her ear.

It was only after he heard her slow, easy breathing, indicating that she had fallen asleep, that he closed his eyes to sleep as well.

Ellie shifted in bed a few times before opening her eyes to a darkened room. She pulled herself up in bed and glanced over at the clock. It was nearly seven at night. Had she slept that long?

And where was Uriel? Had he gone back to his place? Was he downstairs eating spaghetti? She then remembered she had left her laptop still on and sitting on the coffee table. Would he, out of curiosity, see what she was working on? What if he used it to check his e-mail, and noticed the document she was working on?

Not sure of any of those things, she eased out of bed

and slid into her robe. She was halfway down the stairs when she heard his voice, loud and angry. She frowned, wondering who he was talking to. She reached the bottom stair and could see him, fully dressed and standing in her kitchen, talking on his cell phone. He'd said he wasn't involved with anyone, but that didn't mean women wouldn't call him. Was he having an argument with an old girlfriend?

Deciding it was really none of her business, and that he deserved to have his conversation in private, she turned to go back up the stairs, when his next words stopped her in her tracks.

"For God's sake, Mom, for once will you think of someone other than yourself? Don't you know every time you hurt Dad, you're hurting me, too?"

Ellie lifted a brow. He was talking to his mother? Mrs. Lassiter? She heard the pain in his voice and also the frustration. Immediately her heart went out to him.

"Look, Mom, this conversation isn't going anywhere. You just refuse to understand what I'm saying. I'll talk to you later. Goodbye."

A part of Ellie wanted to go to Uriel, hold him and tell him everything would be all right, but he might not want that. That would be getting into his business, and until he invited her into it, she had to remain on the outside.

Ellie turned to head back up the stairs, and when she got to the top she eased down to sit on the step. She heard the back door open and close, indicating he had either left or gone outside to get some fresh air. Again she fought the urge to go to him, get him to talk about it.

She was about to get up and go back into her bedroom, when she heard the back door open and close again and then, moments later, Uriel rounded the corner from the kitchen and glanced up and saw her sitting on the top stair.

He didn't say anything. He just stood there and stared up at her, and even then she felt his anger, but knew it wasn't directed at her. Ellie's natural instinct, the one that loved him, had always loved him, told her to go to him, risk having him tell her she was overstepping the bounds of what was permissible in their affair.

She decided to take the risk anyway, and slowly began walking down the stairs to him. When she reached the bottom step and stood directly in front of him, she wrapped her arms around him and leaned up on tiptoes and joined her mouth to his.

He reciprocated her kiss, reached out and placed his arms around her waist as he eased her closer to him. His hands stroked her back and her backside, while his mouth mated totally and thoroughly with hers.

She gasped when he swept her off her feet and into his arms and headed toward the sofa, sat down and cradled her in his arms. He said nothing for a long time, just sat there holding her, with his chin resting atop her head.

She decided to break his silence by looking up at him and asking, "Are you okay?"

He didn't say anything for a moment, just continued to look down at her, and then he pulled her back into his arms, rested his chin atop her head again and said, "I want to believe that my mother at some point did love my father, but at times, I'm really not sure."

She gave his words a chance to float around them,

and then she asked another question, one whose purpose was to make him think. "Why would you even believe that she didn't?" she asked quietly.

He shifted her in his lap so he could meet her gaze, and then, in a quiet tone, said, "Because she is hurting him so much now. And I can't imagine that a woman who professed to loving a man at one point, could deliberately hurt him the way she is doing. My father left the country this weekend because they were invited to the same party at the country club, and he knew she would be bringing her boy-toy. She parades him around like he's the best thing to happen to her since gingerbread. My father still loves her. Nearly had a nervous breakdown when she asked for a divorce."

Ellie didn't know what to say. She had heard bits and pieces of the story from her aunt and her parents, but she hadn't known how deeply the divorce had affected Mr. Lassiter. And she could clearly see the divorce had affected Uriel as well. She had a question to ask him, mainly because she needed to know.

"Is that the reason you won't consider ever marrying, Uriel? Because of what's happened to your parents' marriage?"

He didn't say anything for a long moment, and she wondered if he would reply. Finally he said, "Yes. I saw my father hurt. I felt his pain. I saw a strong and confident man nearly reduced to a whimpering, poor soul because of his love for a woman, and I made up my mind never to let it happen to me. No woman would ever touch my life that deeply or make me love her that strongly for that to happen. I refuse to let it."

Ellie couldn't say anything. He had pretty much told her in no uncertain terms, that no matter how enjoyable he found her in bed, no matter how much he might take pleasure in her company, when it was time for him to leave Cavanaugh Lake, he would do so without looking back, and possibly, as time passed he wouldn't bother looking her up. If their paths crossed, she would have been just another woman from his past.

"How can I still love her for what she's putting him through, Ellie?"

His question, since he'd asked, was one she felt she could answer. She shifted so she could reach up and place her arms around his neck. "You love her because she is your mom," she said simply. "Our parents don't always do what we want them to do, just like, as their children, we don't always do what they want us to do. We love them anyway, and they love us anyway. Sounds like she's going through a midlife crisis, and it's sad they aren't going through it together."

Her parents certainly had, she thought, remembering how her parents, who didn't even own bicycles, had gone out and purchased his and hers Harleys. And if that wasn't bad enough, they'd joined a motorcycle club and traveled with a group on their motorcycles to Bike Week in Daytona every year. Once she'd gotten over the shock and saw how much fun they were having, she left them alone to do their thing.

"I asked her that, but she said Dad was too busy, never paid any attention to her, because he was working so much. Too bad she couldn't appreciate that he was working so hard to continue to give her the things she'd always wanted. My mother never worked a day in her life. She has a college degree she never used. I never knew how selfish she could be until now."

Ellie said nothing, she just relaxed in his arms and let him vent. It seemed there was a lot he needed to get off his chest. Moments later, when he was finished, he sat there and held her, and she sat there glad to be held. She looked up at him. "Did you get something to eat?"

He nodded. "Yes. Thanks. The spaghetti was good, by the way."

She smiled. "Thank you."

"You're welcome."

She glanced over at the window and saw it had gotten dark outside. She wondered if he would be staying for the night or if he would return to his home. As if he read her thoughts, he leaned closer to her ear and asked in a whisper, "May I spend the night?"

She twisted around in his arms again, and gently pushed him back against the sofa cushion, to sprawl her body over his. She smiled up at him and said, "Yes, you may," before leaning up and placing her mouth on his.

In sleep, Ellie shifted her body to snuggle closer to him, and instinctively, Uriel tightened his arms around her. At least one of them was getting some rest, he thought, as he glanced around the room. They had left a small lamp on near the bedside. He had wanted to see her face while they'd made love. He had wanted to watch how pleasure infused her features when she came. Seeing it would make him explode inside of her, permeate her insides with the essence of him, and she would use her muscles to clamp tight on him, refusing to let him go until she was sure she'd gotten the very last drop.

The thought of a woman wanting that much of him, the thought of wanting to give a woman that much of himself clamored his senses; but then there was nothing about their relationship that was even close to what he was accustomed to with a woman. He had talked about his parents to her. Granted, she knew them, but still, he had told her things he would never have shared with another woman.

And she had listened. He had a feeling that, deep down, she truly cared. Ellie had offered words of encouragement regarding his father. The main thing he should do now was just hope that his father continued to get involved in things. His dad had agreed to go with them to the next NASCAR race in Indianapolis, and that was good. Another good thing was that he would be spending time with Zion this week.

At thirty, Zion was the youngest of the godsons and the one everyone thought needed the most attention, mainly because Zion was considered the loner, the one who would go for months without staying in touch.

The five godbrothers understood and respected Zion's need for privacy when he was working on his jewelry pieces. Unfortunately the godfathers most often did not. When one would show up unexpectedly, interrupting Zion's work flow, he would be quick to put them to work. Uriel could only smile at the thought that his father was sitting somewhere soldering jewelry pieces at this very minute. At least it would keep his old man's mind occupied for a while.

Another thing Donovan had suggested was that his father start dating. If his mother was all wrapped up in someone, then maybe his father should find someone, too. But preferably, unlike his mother, who'd basically gone and robbed the cradle, he'd choose someone closer to his age. Donovan's cousin Vanessa had hinted at introducing his father to her widowed mother. He'd seen Vanessa's mother, and he would be the first to admit that the lady was very attractive. And Anthony Lassiter, at fifty-five, was a good looking man who kept himself in excellent physical shape.

Ellie shifted again and whispered his name, but he quashed the urge to wake her up and make love to her again. He'd certainly made up for not having slept with her last night. They had ended up making love on the sofa downstairs, and then had come back upstairs to make love again. And he had enjoyed each and every moment of it.

But he didn't want to dominate all her time during the coming days, and wasn't into her dominating his, especially since he still had a lot of reading about his publishing company to do. Evidently, she had completed whatever it was she'd been reading. He would spend the night, and tomorrow he would return to his place for awhile and do a few things over there. Five men could get pretty damn sloppy, even in one day, and he needed to clean up the place.

"Uri?"

He glanced down and saw her sleepy eyes staring up at him. "Did my moving around wake you up?" he asked in a low tone.

"No. I woke up on my own." A smile touched her lips. "And now, since I am awake," she said, pushing him back among the pillows and straddling her body over his, "I might as well take advantage of it."

And she did.

Chapter 15

Uriel paused in taking the fish off the hook and glanced over at Ellie. "What do you mean you don't know how to clean fish?" The two of them had gone fishing, and he couldn't believe, he refused to believe what she'd just said.

She shrugged. "I mean what I said. No one has ever taught me. When my dad and I used to fish he would clean them. The times I went fishing with you and your godbrothers, you all would do all the cleaning. There was no need for me to learn."

Uriel squinted his eyes against the brightness of the sun. "Well, I hate to be the bearer of bad news, but there is a need now. We both clean the fish we catch. I believe in equal opportunity."

He couldn't help but laugh at the face she made at him before turning and prancing off the pier and walking toward her house, giving him a delectable view of her backside in a pair of shorts.

"And just where do you think you're going, hot pants?" he called out to her.

She turned around with her chin lifted in the air and said, "Home. I don't want to play with you anymore. I'm going to take a shower and relax. Later, after you've cleaned *all* the fish, come join me."

He lifted a brow. "Umm, and what do I get?"

"What you've been getting all week," she replied bluntly, before turning around and continuing her walk home.

Uriel couldn't help the huge smile that touched his lips. Damn, had it been a full week already? Actually, it had been more than a week. Ten days, to be exact, and the woman had proven to be temptation and enticement all rolled into one.

Nothing was going as he'd planned. He'd thought he could leave her during the day and just show up at night for sex, but things weren't quite working out that way. He'd tried it the first day, but now he was looking in her face 24/7. And he liked being inside her body, as well. He hadn't missed a day making love to her since his god-brothers' departure, alternating between his bed and hers.

They had taken out the time to go fishing, and she had helped him when he'd decided his living room needed a new coat of paint. They had done a movie night over at his place. He'd even been helping her pack up her aunt's belongings in between bouts of lovemaking. Hell, they made love all the time and he was enjoying the hell out of it. But then they would sit down and talk as well. She told him about how she was thinking about going into business for herself, but wasn't sure if that would be the right move. She even mentioned just hanging out at the lake house a few more months before getting back into the workforce. And because he had been in the corporate world a lot longer than she had, he'd given her advice on what companies to avoid. One thing he liked was that she listened and asked questions. Bottom line was that he enjoyed her company both in and out of bed.

Picking up both of their fishing rods as well as the bucket filled with the fish they'd caught, he made it back over to his place. He placed the fish in the sink and grabbed a beer out of the fridge, deciding he would cool down before cleaning the fish. Then he would take a shower and go find Ellie, and when he found her he would—

The ringing of his cell phone interrupted his thoughts, but that was okay, since he knew exactly what he would do to her. He pulled his cell phone out of the back pocket of his shorts. "Yes?"

"Hey, Uri, this is Donovan. I'm a new uncle again. Morgan and his wife Lena just had a son. He came out looking like a slugger. I bet he weighed every bit of ten pounds."

For the next few minutes, he and Donovan talked about the new baby and how the parents were handling things. And then Donovan asked, "How's the fishing? They still biting pretty good?"

"Yes. You ought to grab your fishing rod and come down a few days." Since Donovan had never met Ellie, he wouldn't feel inclined to protect her honor like his godbrothers had. But Uriel had made up his mind about a few things this week. No matter who else showed up at the lake—except for her parents or his, as a matter of respect—he didn't intend on spending a single night out of her bed.

For him to be involved in an affair was commonplace to Donovan, and he wouldn't think anything unusual. With Ellie living next door, Donovan would only think of it as convenient. Before Natalie had come into Donovan's life, he'd been Charlotte's number-one player. In a way, Uriel still couldn't believe Donovan had given all of it up. Just for one woman.

"Donovan, I need to ask you something," he said, when both confusion and curiosity got the best of him.

"Sure. What?"

Uriel knew that although he and Donovan were thick as thieves, were more brothers than friends, he still wanted to word his question carefully. He didn't want to offend anyone or give the impression Donovan had made one hell of a mistake. But his engagement was still too mind-boggling to think about, and Uriel needed his friend to explain why.

"This thing with you and Natalie. The two of you just met last month. She's a gorgeous woman and a nice person to boot. I liked her off the bat, but you've dated a lot of women—lookers, stunners, women so attractive I could weep with envy. Just think of all the booty calls you're giving up. My question to you is, is it—"

"Worth it?" Donovan finished for him.

Uriel released a long and deep breath. "Yes, is it worth it?"

Donovan didn't say anything for a moment, and then he said, "I wish I could explain it, Uriel, but I doubt if I can. And to answer your question, yes, it's worth it. *She* is worth it. I didn't think I would say that about any woman. You know my philosophy. There were too many out there to settle on just one. Being inside the body of one was no different than being inside the body of another. But I found out that isn't true. There is a difference when something comes into the mix you don't expect. Love. Damn, man, it was the weirdest thing. I think I fell in love with Natalie the moment I met her, and one of these days real soon I'm going to have to tell you all about it. You won't believe how we actually met. And although I thought it was all about sex, and once I took her to bed that would be that, I found out it wasn't. There is a difference, and if you ever meet a woman—the woman who is wearing your name somewhere on her heart—you will know. Maybe not right away, but eventually you will."

Uriel thought about what Donovan was saying. If he didn't know his friend as the man he was, as the player he had been, Uriel would think he was nothing more than a lovesick puppy. But he knew that wasn't the case. Donovan hadn't been out there looking for love. He had been doing what he usually did when it came to women, which was looking for sex. But now he was making plans to spend the rest of his life with the same woman, and he actually seemed happy about it. Uriel could not detect one ounce of regret in his voice.

"Like I said, Uriel, you'll know her."

Uriel frowned, deciding not to waste time telling his

friend it wouldn't happen to him. That even if he met this woman, whose name he was supposedly wearing on his heart, he would wonder if she would eventually do to him the same thing his mother had done to his father. The thought of losing his mind over a woman was something he refused to consider.

"I know you met Natalie that one time at the Racetrack Café, but I'd love to bring her down to the lake to spend time with you. How about a fish fry next weekend?" Donovan was saying.

Uriel smiled. He had no problem getting out the fryer again. "Sounds like a great idea, and you and Natalie can have the whole house to yourself for the weekend."

"And where will you be?" Donovan asked.

"Next door. The woman next door and I are...friends," he said, knowing Donovan would get his drift.

"Oh, okay. If you're sure it's okay, I'll make certain Natalie will be available for next weekend. I'll call you later today and let you know."

"All right."

After hanging up the phone and placing it back in his pocket, Uriel still felt a bit confused, as well as somewhat curious. Maybe seeing Donovan and Natalie interact would help him understand the gist of it all. The one and only time he'd seen them together they'd been at odds with each other, and the only thing Uriel had felt flowing between them were tension and anger, at least from Natalie. Donovan had simply come across as frustrated.

Oh, well, he thought, as he went to work cleaning the fish, love and marriage might be for some people, but it definitely wasn't for him.

* * *

A just-showered, fully relaxed Ellie slumped down in her favorite chair by the window, with her laptop in her hand, ready to write a couple of scenes today. And from where she was sitting, she'd be able to see Uriel when he left his house to come to hers.

She began typing, and as if she were in another world, one filled with love and passion, she brought life once again to Grant and Tamara. Her hands seemed to flow over the keys, knowing what they were about to say before they said it.

Moments later, when Ellie finally got to a love scene, she began typing, truly inspired. She and Uriel had been sharing a bed for more than a week and she had never known a more passionate man. Her cheeks couldn't help but color with a blush just thinking about their nights as well as their mornings. And it just wasn't in the things he did, but also the things he said. The man took pillow talk to a whole other level.

She wasn't aware just how long she'd sat there typing, when she heard the sound of a door slamming shut. She glanced up and saw Uriel step off his porch and head over to her place. He glanced up and saw her sitting by the window and smiled before waving at her. She smiled back, noting he had showered and changed clothes.

Ellie shut down her laptop, but not before noting just how much she'd typed. She smiled, pleased with her accomplishment for the day. And she was pleased with how things were going between her and Uriel. It was pretty nice waking up in a man's arms every morning, after falling asleep once she'd been thoroughly made love to at night.

Then there were the other things they did together, like cook breakfast and dinner. He helped her pack up the last of her aunt's belongings to give away and had helped store in the attic those things she wanted to keep. He had driven her into town to a nursery to purchase a couple of fruit trees she wanted for the backyard, and had even chopped wood for the winter months; if she decided to come back later in the year, there would be enough ready for the fireplace. And he had made watching movies with him special.

Sensations suddenly overwhelmed her at the thought that in two weeks he would be leaving Cavanaugh Lake to return to Charlotte. Their affair would be ending. She would remain here and finish the book, which shouldn't take too long. Then she would return to Boston. She had decided to wait until the first of the year to decide if she wanted to go back into corporate America, or start her own business. Uriel had given her good advice regarding the pros and cons of both.

She didn't have to look up to know he had entered the bedroom. She felt his presence. She was intercepting his heat. She knew, at that moment when they went their separate ways, her pain would be almost too much to bear, but she would. She had no choice.

Tilting her head back, she stared at him. He was leaning in the doorway, shirtless and wearing a pair of shorts that, in her opinion, looked just as scandalous as any she'd ever worn. They displayed just what a good physique he had: flat stomach; muscular thighs; strong legs. And a thick arousal pressing hard against his crotch. It wouldn't be so bad if she didn't know what was behind the shorts. She knew every solid inch of him there, had seen it erect and nonerect. Her fingers had touched it, gently squeezed it, had given it her own personal massage. And one night, in a surprise move and with a bold degree of naughtiness, her mouth had tasted it, almost greedily, and several satisfied groans had escaped his lips. She now knew all the things that brought him pleasure, all the ways they could be done, what it took to push him over the edge, make him call out her name in a throaty growl. Remembering made an intense shudder ripple down her spine.

She had opened the bedroom window earlier, and a gentle breeze was coming in, stirring the heat he was emitting, as well as his scent. The air between them seemed to spark, and she had a feeling if she didn't say something, didn't start conversation, they were liable to go up in flames just from staring across the room at each other. So to break the silence, she asked, "Did you get all the fish cleaned?"

"Yes, with no help from you."

She couldn't help but chuckle. "You poor baby. Do you want some cheese to go with that whine?"

"Do you really want to know what I want, Ellie?"

"No," she said, managing a faint smile, letting her gaze travel back down to his crotch, then back to his face. "I have an idea."

A smile curved his lips. "And you're probably right. But I can wait till after dinner for you to be my dessert," he said, coming into the room. "Besides, we need to talk."

She raised a brow. "About what?"

"More company coming. My business partner, Donovan Steele. I think I mentioned he'd gotten engaged."

She nodded. "Yes, you did."

"Well, I invited him and his fiancée to come to Cavanaugh Lake for the weekend for a fish fry."

"This weekend?"

He chuckled. "No, next weekend. I haven't forgotten my promise to take you rafting in the Smokies this weekend."

"Good."

"And I hope you don't mind, but I gave them full use of my place for the weekend, which means I'll be crashing over here," he said.

"No, I don't mind," she responded. He'd been crashing at her place anyway. Since their affair had begun, the only night he hadn't stayed was the one night his godbrothers had come to visit.

"How would you like to take a walk before we get into the kitchen to fix dinner?"

"A walk?" She'd said it like she hadn't heard him right.

He grinned. "Yes, a walk. When was the last time you actually walked around Cavanaugh Lake, all the way to the east bank?"

"Too long ago to remember. Why the interest in doing so now?" She was curious enough to ask.

He leaned back against the dresser and said, "I'm thinking of buying a boat, nothing too big, but it's something I've always wanted. I want to walk to the other side of the lake to make sure that old dock is still there. If it's not, I'm going to have to build one."

She nodded. "If it's there, you might need to get it repaired," she pointed out.

"No problem. So put on a pair of good shoes and let's go," he said, moving toward the door.

She laughed and gave him a hearty salute. "Yes, boss."

He turned around and gave her a charming smile. "I'm not your boss."

"Oh, then what are you?" she asked sweetly.

His gaze seemed clouded in an arousing heat when he said, "Your lover."

He was her *lover*.

Uriel made a mental acknowledgment of the words he had spoken to Ellie earlier that day. That acknowledgment was followed by an image that popped into his mind. It was a scene that had taken place less than an hour ago, right in his bed, before Ellie had drifted off to sleep. It was one that affirmed his claim. Proven without a shadow of a doubt. He was her lover.

Even now, they were lying facing each other, her head resting snugly on his chest, their legs entwined, and their bodies still intimately connected. He felt himself getting hard again, just thinking about how things had started out with her being his dessert in the kitchen, and his late-night snack in the bedroom. And he had basically been hers.

He slid his arms around her, opening his hands on her bottom, to pull her snugly against him for an even better connection when he felt himself starting to get hard again. His shaft was happy, very contented, because it was where it wanted to be. It would probably protest if he were to pull out of her. A satisfied groan flowed from his lips. *He* was happy and very content as well.

He glanced over at the nightstand at the several packets of condoms. Although he placed them there every night, he had yet to use one. With Ellie, he enjoyed the feel of skin-to-skin, flesh-to-flesh. He enjoyed the feel of exploding inside of her, jetting his hot release into her—something he had never considered doing to another woman. She was on the Pill, but then, every once in awhile, when the possibility did cross his mind, he would envision a prissy little girl with skin the color of Ellie's and eyes identical to his. And just like all the other times when such foolish images formed in his mind, he was quick to dismiss them. He felt his shaft grow even harder inside of her and tried like hell to ignore it. No luck. A shudder ran down his body, rippling along his spine, electrifying the hard muscles in his erection.

She must have felt it. She must have felt *him*. Not surprisingly, since he was stretching her again to accommodate his growing manhood. She slowly opened her eyes and met his. She smiled and gave him a sleepy but knowing look.

"Sorry," he apologized. "I didn't mean to wake you, but I guess my friend wants attention." And as he felt himself grow larger still, he added, "No regrets."

She smiled as he held tight to her body, remaining inside of her as he turned and placed her on top of him. She gazed down at him and said, "And that's why your friend and I like each other so much, and why we get along so well—because I have no regrets, either. We don't have time to waste, since it will be the end of the month before you know it."

Her words reminded him of just how true that was. It would be the end of the month soon, and he didn't want to waste time. He wanted to savor every moment that he could with her, because when it ended, it ended. But for now, he was wrapping his arms around her as she began riding him as if her very life depended on it, moving up and down, permeating the air with her scent, his scent, the aroma of their lovemaking. He had this.

His jaw tightened each time he lifted himself to meet her downward movement. This was the best of the best, the cream of the crop, off the charts. This is what made a man appreciate being a man…and what made a man appreciate having a good woman.

He tossed that very claim out of his mind. This woman was his *temporarily*. By rights, she should be doing all the things she'd done to him, and with him, for the past ten days to a man who would be a permanent part of her future. A man who would flood her body with his seed to make babies, a man she could commit her life to, as he would commit his to her. A man who would not place a limit on the time they spent together.

He was not that man; but for now, tonight, until the end of the month, they could both pretend.

Chapter 16

"And Donovan, this is Ellie."

Uriel watched Donovan's expression when he turned his attention to the woman by his side. Surprise, confusion and keen interest were showing in Donovan Steele's gaze, but only someone as close to Donovan as Uriel would be able to detect it. Uriel could just imagine what his friend was thinking. Ellie was beautiful, and for him to even consider eventually walking away would be stone crazy. But then, Uriel knew those were the thoughts of the new, engaged and about-to-be-married Donovan.

The old Donovan would have understood and not questioned his motives or decision. He would have patted him on the back for making such a lucrative score—a worthwhile conquest—and would have given him a wink of envy. But not the Donovan that was deeply in love with the gorgeous woman standing by his side, so much so that he couldn't keep his eyes off of her. *Jeesh.* Uriel figured it was going to take some getting used to this Donovan Steele.

After all the introductions were made, Uriel saw how quickly Ellie and Natalie took to each other like old friends. When the conversation between them shifted to a subject he was certain neither he nor Donovan gave a royal damn about—namely the right shampoo and conditioner to keep the frizz out of your hair in this August heat—he caught Donovan's attention and rolled his eyes, before saying, "I'll help you get the luggage out of the car."

The two women went inside his house while he and Donovan went to the back of the car to open the trunk. Uriel raised a brow when he saw several pieces of luggage. "Hey, Don, you and Natalie are here just for the weekend, not for the rest of the year, right?"

Donovan chuckled. "Natalie wasn't sure what to pack, so she tucked in a little of everything."

Uriel gave him a wry look, knowing how Donovan detested excessiveness in anyone…or at least, he used to. "And you're still going to marry her with this one major flaw?" he asked teasingly.

Donovan threw his head back and laughed. "In a heartbeat. Tomorrow, if she'd agree to it. Hell, I tried, at a weak moment, getting her to fly to Vegas with me, but she refused."

Uriel shook his head. "I guess you're going to have to work harder on her."

"Just like Ellie is going to have to work harder on you?"

Uriel raised a brow, and tried to keep his body from stiffening at Donovan's words. "Meaning?"

"She likes you."

Uriel relaxed somewhat. "And I like her. But nothing is going to keep me from ending our relationship in eight days."

"Then I hope you know what you're doing."

Uriel gave his friend another wry look, wondering if Donovan realized what he was suggesting. A serious relationship, one that could end in marriage, babies, and a little house with a picket fence was nowhere in his future, and Donovan, of all people, knew that.

Deciding it was time to change the subject, Uriel asked, "How are things going with the Steele Corporation? I understand you had a serious internal issue."

"Everything is fine. Fortunately, we identified the person trying to give company secrets to our competitor. A man in Morgan's department who'd worked with us for years. I'm glad we made the discovery before he could do any damage."

Donovan then asked, "So, how does our publishing company look?"

Uriel knew that the reason Donovan was asking had nothing to do with the possibility that they'd made a wrong investment. That wasn't the case, since they had checked out Vandellas Publishing thoroughly before making the purchase. It had been financially sound. Their main concern was making sure it remained a viable acquisition over the next three years, until they were ready to sell.

"I haven't finished going through all the documents as I'd planned."

"I can understand why," Donovan said, with a smirk on his face.

Uriel ignored him and said, "But I plan to do so this week. I'm anxious to go over their inventory lists to see how many books they published this year, and how many they plan to publish next year. I'm also curious to see who they gave high advances to and what promotional and marketing strategies they intend to use to make sure those books sell."

They carried the luggage to the door and when they entered they could hear Ellie and Natalie chatting away. He glanced over at Donovan. "They're still talking about hair products?"

Donovan grinned. "Sounds like it."

"Then we need to pull them apart and give them something else to talk about, don't you think?" Uriel said, winking at his friend.

Three days later, Ellie eased out of bed, thinking that this past weekend had been fun spending time with Donovan and Natalie, and in a way, she'd regretted seeing them leave. While Donovan had helped Uriel fry the fish, Natalie had helped her make coleslaw. And for dessert, Natalie had offered to make her aunt's mouthwatering peach cobbler. That meant going to the grocers and getting all the ingredients they needed. During the drive, Natalie told Ellie her and Donovan's love story and filled her in on their June wedding plans.

It only took being around the couple for a brief period of time to see how much in love they were. Ellie couldn't help but wonder how it would feel to be loved that much by any man, to know that you, of all women, had been the one he chose to be with for the rest of his life, to be cherished by him, deeply loved to the point where he would want you to be the mother of his babies, the woman he wanted to make love to for the rest of his days.

Ellie glanced back over her shoulder at Uriel, who was sprawled out naked on top of the mattress, heart-stoppingly breathtaking. From the way his erection was growing before her eyes, he was getting aroused all over again. "Make it go down," she ordered, and couldn't help but giggle as she slipped into the shorts he had removed last night.

Uriel's hand, the one that had been thrown over his eyes to ward off the morning sun coming through the window, slid down just enough to look over at her. "You come back to bed and *make* it go down, because I sure as hell can't. When it wants you, even a cold shower won't work."

Ellie figured there was no use reminding Uriel that *it* had had her several times during the night. But what she *would* remind him was that he'd promised to take her to dinner at that Italian restaurant in Gatlinburg. They were winding down the time they would be spending together, because in four days he would leave to return to Charlotte.

She glanced over at the bed and saw that Uriel had drifted back off to sleep. Would he ever give his heart a chance to share a love such as Natalie's and Donovan's? Or would he let what happened with his parents' marriage be the reason he would never want that kind of love, that kind of relationship, for himself? And for that very reason, she would never let him know just how much she loved him, just how much her heart would break in a few days when he would be leaving, going back to a world without her in it.

She slowly walked over to the bed, leaned down and placed a kiss on his lips. She then glanced around his bedroom, saw a pen and a piece of paper lying on the dresser, and scribbled a note, letting him know she was going back to her place to shower, and to then start packing the last of her aunt's things.

A short while later, back at her place, and after taking a shower and putting on her favorite shorts set, Ellie headed downstairs, wondering if Uriel was still in his bed asleep. He had mentioned last night that he would be spending the first part of the morning finishing up reading about some company he and Donovan had purchased a month or so ago.

She had just taken the milk out of the refrigerator for her cereal when the house phone rang. She lifted a brow, wondering who would be calling this early on a Monday morning. Most people she knew called her on her cell phone, which meant the caller was probably one of those telemarketers. She decided not to pick it up, but changed her mind, thinking it could possibly be her parents.

"Hello?"

"Is Mable Weston there?"

Ellie frowned. Most people who knew her aunt were aware she'd passed away. "May I ask who's calling?"

"Yes, this is Lauren Poole."

It didn't take long for Ellie to recall the name, and she leaned back against the refrigerator in surprise, quickly remembering that the last time her back had been against the refrigerator Uriel had pinned her there.

"Hello. Are you there?"

The woman's voice pulled her thoughts back to the conversation and the realization of just who Lauren Poole was. "Yes, I'm here."

"May I speak with Mable please?"

Ellie gnawed nervously on her bottom lip before saying, "Sorry, she's resting." She breathed in deeply, while thinking that it wasn't really a complete lie. "This is her niece, Ellie Weston. Is there something I can help you with?"

"Oh, yes, her niece. Mable speaks of you often. She simply adores you."

"Thanks. And I adore her as well. Is there a message you'd like to leave? I'll be happy to make sure she gets it." Now *that,* Ellie thought, *was* a lie.

"I just wanted to let her know that the Vandellas Publishing Company was sold to another company, but the buyout changes nothing, as it relates to her contract. She still has until the end of the year to turn in the manuscript, and the release date for the book is still July of next year."

Ellie nodded her head, thinking that was good to hear. "I appreciate you calling and will make sure she gets your message."

"Thank you. I'm looking forward to receiving the finished manuscript, and so is her editor at Vandellas. We all thought it was a beautiful romance, and we're eager to get more stories by Flame Elbam."

Ellie drew in a deep breath. Now was the perfect

time to tell Lauren Poole that her aunt had died, and that there was no way Aunt Mable, aka Flame Elbam, would supply them with more manuscripts. "Ms. Poole."

"Yes?"

Ellie opened her mouth to tell the woman the truth, but closed it when she recalled the words her aunt had written in the letter Mr. Altman had given to her. Although the publishing company and Ms. Poole probably wouldn't think so, Ellie believed she was doing the right thing by completing her aunt's novel.

"Yes, Miss Weston?"

"Nothing. I'll give Aunt Mable the message."

"Thank you."

After the phone conversation ended, Ellie drew in a deep breath and then slowly released it. She was doing what her aunt would have wanted. And she knew that, in addition to Uriel's inspiration, her aunt was inspiring her as well. There was no way she could have gotten into the characters so deeply over the past three weeks without her aunt's divine intervention. So she truly believed she was finishing the manuscript with her aunt's blessing.

But what about Uriel's?

Ellie went over to the table and sat down. He had only inspired her because she loved him. To him, this summer fling may have been about nothing but sex, but to her it had been so much more. Every time he had touched her, she fell deeper and deeper in love with him, and she knew that the day he left to return to Charlotte would be the hardest day of her life.

But she wanted him to leave knowing the truth.

Although the past three weeks were nothing but an affair for him, she wanted him to know that for her it had meant something more.

Chapter 17

Uriel lay in bed and stared up at the ceiling. In four days he would be leaving this place to return to Charlotte. When he pulled out of the driveway on Sunday evening, he would look straight ahead, wonder how well his assistant had managed things in his absence, and look forward to getting back into the swing of things at Lassiter Industries.

He would not dwell on what he'd been doing for the past three weeks, the summer fling he thoroughly enjoyed. Why would he? It had been nothing more than an affair, and affairs were insignificant. After one ended, you rested up, gave yourself breathing room and prepared for the next one. Life moved on.

Then why did he suddenly feel like his was standing still?

Why did the thought of leaving here, not seeing Ellie, not spending time with her, not making love to her, leave an emptiness in his stomach, a vacant spot in his chest surrounding his heart?

An unfamiliar feeling stirred in his gut, and he tried shoving it away. Instead, it moved to his shoulder blades and then to the lower part of his back. Agonized, he closed his eyes, and the only image that could form behind his closed eyelids was Ellie. He saw her as she'd looked that night she had stood at her window, stripping for him, giving him her decision to have an affair with him in a style that even now left him breathless.

And then Ellie as she had looked later when he had entered her, felt her tightness squeeze him, and her wetness surround him, flesh-to-flesh, skin-to-skin.

He saw too the Ellie who had spent the past three weeks with him, making him enjoy a woman's company in a way he'd never done before. Sharing breakfast with her, going fishing with her, going skinny-dipping with her, watching movies till dawn with her, making impromptu love to her, anytime and anyplace—tasting her with a hunger and need that he hadn't experienced with any woman. And having unprotected sex with her and enjoying shooting his seed into her, while actually imagining the baby they could be making together.

He thought of Ellie, and those times she held him within her body, clenched him with a need that could make him come. How she would stroke him, take him into her mouth and love him that way, and how he would doze off to sleep, wanting her near him, with his hands between her legs to keep her there. Before now he refused to believe there was a difference in passion. Now he knew there was lovemaking passion and sex passion. The passion that flowed through his body whenever he was inside of Ellie was lovemaking passion.

He opened his eyes and stared at the ceiling again, as his heart began to pound deep in his chest and every bone in his body began to quiver. There could be only one reason for him feeling as he did. One reason he needed to finally face up to.

He then recalled Donovan's words of just a few days ago: "If you ever meet the woman who is wearing your name somewhere on her heart—you will know."

He knew. He knew at that very moment that it was Ellie's name scrawled on his heart. *Damn*. He eased out of bed, thinking he needed a beer, then deciding a shot of whiskey—preferably Jack Daniel's—would do better. How had he allowed himself to fall in love, after what his mother had done to his father? Was he a glutton for the same type of experience?

He knew that the only thing he was a glutton for was Ellie. She was not like his mother. He would be able to put all his love and trust in her and not be betrayed.

He rubbed his hand over his face. His shower could wait. He needed to see Ellie, and he needed to see her now.

Ellie released a long sigh and wondered why she had called Darcy, when she knew what her best friend would say. "I hear what you're saying, Darcy, but a part of me feels I should come clean and tell Uriel the truth. And if you think it won't matter, then fine. I just don't want him to think these past three weeks meant nothing to me."

"Okay, El, if you think that's what you should do, then fine, do it. But if he's like most men, all that matters with an affair is the outcome, and the outcome was three weeks in his bed. I doubt he would have given that up for anything."

"Maybe not, Darcy, but the bottom line is that I got a call from my aunt's literary agent, to tell me that Vandellas Publishing was sold to another company. I'm glad Uriel was around so I could get plenty of lovemaking inspiration to finish the book for her as Flame Elbam. But the bottom line is that, when he finds out he is going to know that he was being used."

Suddenly, she thought she heard a noise outside, and glanced out the window but didn't see anything. She then pulled in a deep breath and said, "That's why I have to tell him the truth. I have to let him know that he wasn't used. That I love him, and the time I spent with him was special."

She took a deep breath, and was grateful that, for once, Darcy didn't say anything.

"Look, Darcy, I have to go. I have a lot to do before Uriel comes over. And then I will tell him the truth. Everything. He deserves that."

Somehow, Uriel made it back to his house and dropped down in his kitchen chair, while the words he had heard Ellie speak rang so clear in his mind.

He had been about to knock on her back door, when two names she'd spoken grabbed him. Darcy and Vandellas Publishing. Darcy was her best friend, the one who'd talked her into that dare ten years ago, and Vandellas Publishing was the company that he and Donovan now owned. What was Ellie talking about when she said she would finish a book for her aunt for his publishing company? And better yet, how had his lovemaking inspired her to finish the book?

A part of him knew he probably should have just hung around and asked her, demanded a few answers. But the part of him that had just admitted to being in love with her less than an hour ago felt raw and betrayed.

He breathed in deeply as he replayed her words that were still so clear in his mind.

He stood, and slowly walked up the stairs to his bedroom, where he pulled open his briefcase. It didn't take him long to find the papers he was looking for. The first was a detailed listing of all the outstanding manuscripts. He quickly scanned the page and found the name "Flame Elbam," and in parenthesis it showed "Mable Weston."

Uriel blinked. Ms. Mable had been writing one of those romance novels? He pulled in a breath deeply. The woman was in her seventies, for crying out loud, so it had to be one of those sweet and innocent types where the man and woman did nothing more than hold hands, or kiss each other on the cheek.

He nearly swallowed his tongue when, moments later, he saw the category Ms. Mable's book had been purchased for: erotica. The paper he was holding almost slipped out of his hand, and he couldn't do anything but gape his mouth before dropping down on the side of his bed in shock. Sweet little old Ms. Mable had been writing erotica romances? He read farther and saw she'd been given an advance of over fifty thousand dollars.

Damn. First his mother and her boy-toy, and now Ms. Mable and her erotica romances…the female population never ceased to amaze him. His thoughts then shifted to Ellie. There was nothing on the paper he was holding in his hand to indicate that Mable Weston, aka Flame Elbam, would not be turning her manuscript in, which revealed Ellie's devious plan to outwit the publisher and finish the book herself.

Using him for her research.

Anger consumed him at the thought that, once again, ten years later, she and her friend Darcy had played him for a fool. The years hadn't matured them at all. Instead of getting wiser, they had gotten more conniving and deceitful. It would do Darcy justice to one day meet someone like York, who would see through her with the first blink, and then show her no mercy.

But for him, his bone of contention was with Ellie, the woman he had been foolish enough to fall in love with, the woman who had broken his heart before it had gotten a chance to accept that it could beat for one woman.

Deciding he no longer wanted to be within even fifty feet of Ellie, he went to the closet and threw his luggage out on the bed and moved around the room throwing things into it. There was nothing she could say. Nothing he wanted to hear.

She had made a fool of him for the last time.

Ellie climbed the steps to Uriel's front door, surprised to find it cracked open. It was not like him to forget to lock the door behind him. She had expected him to come over to her place at least by noon, and wondered if he was still asleep. She was prepared to tell him everything.

She entered the house, and when she heard him moving around upstairs, she called out to him as she headed toward the stairs, "Uriel, I'm coming up."

"Don't bother."

She looked up at him and saw that he was standing at the top of the stairs staring back. The look on his face sent chills through her body. And he had his luggage in his hand. She swallowed and wondered what was wrong. Had something happened to his father? His mother?

"Uriel, what is it? What happened?"

The laugh that emitted from his throat was just as cold and chilling as the look he was giving her. "You want to know what happened, Ellie? I'll tell you what happened. Stupid me. Foolish me. Wanting to believe, after ten years, you had grown up and had matured, not just in body but also in mind—only to discover that, once again, you and your friend, Darcy decided to play me. This time, using me in the bedroom, since you've outgrown a mere kiss on the pier. You needed to finish your aunt's book, and I was the perfect man to research those bedroom scenes you needed to write."

At the surprised look in her eyes, Uriel laughed again and said, "Yes, I was coming over to see you and just happened to overhear your conversation with your friend Darcy. I heard everything you said. Go play games with someone else, and get out of my house. You aren't welcome here."

"Uriel, please listen. You didn't hear everything, and

I wasn't playing a game with you. I had planned to tell you everything about Aunt Mable's book and—"

"When? When had you planned to tell me, Ellie? Once the book was published, and my name appeared in the acknowledgments as the man who inspired you to write all those lovemaking scenes? The man who introduced you to all those various positions? The man you used once again, ten years later."

"Uriel, I—"

"Please leave. And you can have Cavanaugh Lake all to yourself, because I am going back to Charlotte."

He came down the stairs and stood in front of her. The anger on his face was reflected in his eyes as well, when he said, "Now, please leave so I can lock up the place."

Ellie met his gaze and knew that no matter what she said to him, he would not listen. So she turned and headed for the door. But not before looking back one final time, hoping, just hoping, she would once again see his eyes and a smile curve his lips. She saw neither. Instead, she saw the hard, cold expression of a very angry man. A man who had all but told her he did not, would not, allow her back into his life again.

She turned and walked away, opening the door and then walking out of it. She kept walking, refusing to stop until she was safely inside her own home. And then she made it to the sofa, slumped down and covered her face in her hands. It was only moments later, when she heard the sound of his car pulling away, that she let the tears fall, unheeded, down her face.

Kicking off her sandals, she decided to lie down,

doubting her legs would be able to carry her anywhere right now. And she closed her eyes and cried some more.

Ellie opened her eyes and looked around, and when she glanced out the window she saw that dusk was covering the earth. She pulled herself up, not believing she had actually slept for over five hours.

But she had slept, and while doing so she had dreamed. It had been a pleasant dream, one of her and her aunt. They had laughed and they had talked, and then her aunt had held her while she cried. It had seemed so real, but she knew it had been merely a dream.

Still, she had come away with something very important. Her aunt wanted her to finish the book, and in doing so, she would be stronger when she confronted Uriel again. If he thought he had seen the last of her, he was sadly mistaken. She would give him time to cool his anger, and then she was going to Charlotte to see him. No matter what it took, she would make him realize her aunt's book was a blessing to them and not a curse.

It might have been the reason she'd agreed to an affair with him, but it hadn't been the reason she had fallen in love with him.

Chapter 18

"Have a nice weekend, Mr. Lassiter."

Uriel paused and glanced over his shoulder at his administrative assistant. "Thank you, Karen, and I hope you do the same."

"Are you headed out to your lake place for the Labor Day weekend?" Karen asked, and smiled as he grabbed his briefcase off his desk.

"No. I plan to have a quiet weekend at home."

He quickly left the office, not wanting to engage in any further conversation with Karen, or anyone else for that matter. He'd already seen his father before he'd left for the day. His father had made plans to fly to New York and visit with York and his parents.

Due to the holiday traffic on the road, it took Uriel longer than usual to get home. Normally, he would drop by the Racetrack Café and have a couple of beers with Donovan, Xavier and Bronson. But Bronson was racing this weekend at the Atlanta Motor Speedway, and the guys had gone to Atlanta to give him their support. Uriel thought about going, but had changed his mind. He much preferred being by himself this weekend. Now he knew how his father must have felt. It had been two weeks, and the pain hadn't eased any.

Donovan had accused him of being stubborn and had tried encouraging him to call Ellie, and listen to her—to let her explain her side of things. Donovan had shared with him the mistake he'd made in jumping to conclusions with Natalie. But Uriel's heart had hardened more at the thought of even talking to Ellie.

He let himself inside his home, and again noticed how lonely it seemed. He went into his bedroom, tossed his suit jacket on the bed and decided to slip into a pair of jeans and T-shirt before ordering take-out. Then he intended to spend the rest of the evening, probably the entire weekend, with ESPN.

He was stretched out on the sofa, watching the NFL preseason highlights, when he heard the sound of his doorbell. Thinking it was the pizza delivery man, he grabbed the twenty-dollar bill off the table and walked to the door in his bare feet and opened it.

Instead of the pizza man, Ellie stood there. He had to blink to make sure he wasn't seeing things, and then, with the anger he hadn't manage to cap, said in a cold tone, "What the hell are you doing here?"

Ellie dragged in a deep breath as she gazed into Uriel's eyes. Two weeks hadn't softened them any. They were just as cold as that day he had left Cavanaugh Lake. But she couldn't let that stop her from doing what she needed to do. What she had to do. It would be the same thing Tamara had had to force Grant to do: to listen to her reasons for doing what she'd done, and make him believe, no matter what or how long it took, that every time he had touched her, had made love to her, she had loved him.

And before she left, she would make Uriel face up to the fact that he loved her, too. She truly believed it, and it had taken finishing her aunt's manuscript to realize it. She was not dealing with make-believe, but hard, cold reality. And no man would have handled her the way he had unless he had loved her. She believed that. Once they got their love out in the open, they would be able to handle the rest. The man standing in front of her was her destiny. Now she had to convince him of that.

"I asked what you are doing here, Ellie."

"We need to talk." Before he realized what she was about to do, she slipped past him and walked into his house. She didn't turn around until she was in the middle of his living room, and when she did, the shocked look on his face almost endeared him to her.

"You weren't invited inside my house," he said, slamming the door shut.

"Then put me out," she challenged, knowing he wouldn't. He wouldn't come close to her. He wouldn't touch her. He was so much like Grant Hatteras that her heart ached. That's why the last two chapters had come easily to her, and she had been able to finish them in ten days.

And since she had decided to come clean, before she sent the manuscript to Lauren Poole yesterday, she had called the woman, confessed to what she'd done. Lauren had been more than understanding, and had agreed to read the entire manuscript as soon as she got it. If Lauren felt everything flowed smoothly, and Ellie had been able to capture her aunt's writing voice, then she would notify Vandellas Publishers, and request that they go ahead and print the book as the first and final work of Flame Elbam.

"You have three minutes."

She glanced over at Uriel. "I'm taking five," she said, sitting down on the sofa and crossing her legs. "Ten, if I need them."

She'd seen him glance at her legs when she crossed them. She had him figured out, which was why she had worn this particular skirt with the split in the side. And she wondered if he had picked up on the fact that she didn't have a bra on underneath her blouse. He would find out soon enough.

He stared at her. She stared at him. There were some things a man couldn't hide, no matter how quick he might be to do so, and when he came and quickly sat down in the chair across from her she knew. He might be mad at her, but his body still wanted her.

"I'm waiting."

She pulled in a deep breath and then said, "I don't want you waiting, Uriel, I want you listening. Will you listen to what I have to say?"

"Maybe."

Okay, if he wanted to be difficult, then she would

show him what being difficult was about in a minute, if he kept it up. "I will start at the beginning. I found my aunt's unfinished manuscript…."

Uriel stared at her. Was he listening? Most of the time. The rest of it was spent watching her lips move, watching that tongue work inside her mouth, watching how she nervously twitched her crossed legs, watching her hand gestures. Just plain watching her. And remembering.

Remembering the lips he kissed. The tongue that had mingled with his, the pair of legs he had been between and the hands that had stroked him. He felt his crotch harden. Felt the way his pulse rate increased. Felt the heat that was beginning to run up his spine.

"Uriel?"

He blinked. "What?"

"I asked you a question."

He frowned. Had she? He shifted in the chair. "Could you repeat the question?"

"Sure. I asked whose idea it was for us to have that summer fling?"

His frown deepened, wondering what point she was trying to make. "It was my idea."

"Why?"

"Why?" he repeated.

"Yes, why?" she almost snapped.

A moment of silence was all it took before he said, "Because I wanted you."

A faint smile took shape on her lips, and then she asked, "For what reason?"

For what reason? A lump formed in his throat. Why was she asking all these questions?

"For what reason, Uriel?" she repeated.

He hesitated before replying, then thought, what the hell. He would tell her just what she wanted to know. "Sex," he said, and just in case she didn't hear it, he said it again, louder this time, "*Sex.*"

She was out of her seat in a flash, and he had to draw back when she got in his face. "You're mad at me for wanting you for sex, but you just admitted to wanting me for the same thing. Please explain that!"

Annoyance rushed through him. "There's nothing to explain. It was what it was, and you knew it from the beginning. But *you* had ulterior motives in what you did."

She stared at him, her brows arched and chin tilted. She backed up and returned to stand by the sofa. "I needed to be inspired to finish my aunt's novel. I finished it and I told her agent the truth, and she will tell the publishing company the truth. If the work is acceptable, they will publish it as Flame Elbam."

She didn't say anything for a moment, and then said, "Finishing that manuscript meant a lot to me, Uriel, and I appreciate your giving me what I needed to do it. No man had ever really and truly made love to me before, and I knew you could and would do it right. What was wrong with that?"

He got on his feet, quickly covered the distance separating them, to stand in front of her. He tightened his hands into fists at his sides, or else he'd be tempted to strangle her. He suddenly felt out of control.

Untamed. "What was wrong with it was that you should have told me!"

Refusing to retreat, she dragged in a deep breath and then let it out before asking, "And if I had, Uriel? Would you have done anything differently? Would you have?"

He frowned. "That is not the point."

She threw up her hands in frustration. "And what is the point? You got what you wanted and so did I. In fact, I got more than I ever dreamed of getting, Uriel, because for three weeks I made love to the man I have loved since I knew what love was about, or thought I knew what it was about. Even that day ten years ago, I had this huge crush on you. And I always dreamed you would be the first boy I kissed. I got to share so many firsts with you, as well as seconds, and I don't regret any of it."

She paused, held his gaze and said, "Yes, I wanted you to inspire me. Yes, you did. And yes, maybe I should have told you about it. But you wanted to have an affair with me. You asked and I consented, whatever the reason. You got from me what you wanted. Now I plan to get from you what I want, then I will leave you in peace."

Uriel's mind was too wrapped up in her admission of her love for him to pay attention to what else she was saying. He saw her kick off her shoes, but didn't realize what she was about to do until her hand went to the zipper of her skirt.

"What do you think you're doing, Ellie?"

"What does it look like?"

And with that smart-ass response, her skirt dropped to the floor, leaving her clad in a pair of black lace bikini panties. He frowned at her. "Lady, you've got a lot of nerve."

She threw her head back and laughed. "Glad you think so." She reached out and grabbed his jeans by the waist. Before he could resist, she had pushed him back, and they both went tumbling onto the sofa, with her landing on top of him.

He glared up at her. "Is there anything in particular that you're trying to prove?" he asked, not believing how she was carrying on.

"Yes," she said, holding his gaze. "Let me know when it's starting to work."

And then she lowered her head and kissed him, seducing his mouth with the sweetest pair of lips he had ever known, and then tangling with his tongue. He didn't resist—didn't even try—when their mouths began mating with a hunger that would not be denied.

When she finally pulled her mouth back, she whispered against his lips, "I love you, Uriel. It's always been about love for me. Even when I knew you were going to leave me at the end of the month, I still wanted to be with you because I loved you. You could only inspire me because I loved you."

He stared up at her and then he knew. Her name was still written on his heart. It hadn't gotten erased. It could never get erased. He pushed a wayward strand of hair back from her face, and he studied her features and knew that one day he would have a daughter who would look just like her.

"And I love you, too, Ellie," he said huskily, admitting what he should have figured out long before he actually had. "I realized it before leaving the lake, and I had been headed over to tell you that day when I heard you talking on the phone to Darcy."

She nodded. "Had you hung around and listened to all of the conversation, you would have heard me tell Darcy of my decision to tell you everything because I loved you."

Cupping her behind the neck, he brought her mouth down to meet his, and their tongues mingled in a kiss that was beginning to burn him inside out. He could feel the thudding of her heart against his, and then he realized something, her nipples pressing hard against his chest.

He pulled back. "You're not wearing a bra," he said in disbelief.

Ellie couldn't help but laugh. "No, I'm not. I started not to wear any panties either, but with the split in my skirt, I thought that might be too much. Either way, I'd planned on making you incapable of speech for a while."

Uriel smiled. "What have I created?"

Her features took a serious turn when she said, "A woman who will love you forever."

He reached out and brushed his knuckles against the softness of her cheeks and said, "And I am a man who will love you forever, as well." He kissed her. "There's something I think you ought to know. If I didn't know any better, I'd think your Aunt Mable had a hand in all of this."

She lifted a brow. "In all of what?"

"That publishing company. Vandellas Publishing. Donovan and I own it. I didn't know it was the one that was publishing your aunt's work until I heard you talking with Darcy. Just so you know, I plan to remain impartial. It will be the editor's decision as to whether you did your aunt's manuscript justice. If you did, then it will be published."

Her eyes lit up and she smiled. "And if I did a good job and they want another book from Flame Elbam, would you let me write it?"

He shrugged. "I don't see why not."

"And will you inspire me again?" she asked, leaning in closer and using the tip of her tongue to trace around his lips.

"Baby," he said in a quivering breath, "all you have to do is ask."

"I'm asking."

He stood up and pulled her into his arms. As he quickly moved toward the bedroom, he glanced down at her and smiled. "That's one request that you don't have to make twice."

Epilogue

"How did you manage to get married before I did?" a disgruntled Donovan Steele asked Uriel, as the two stood with Uriel's five godbrothers for another wedding picture.

Uriel rolled his eyes and remembered something Ellie had once asked him. "Would you like some cheese to go along with your whine?"

Donovan frowned. "Funny."

Uriel shook his head. "Hey, at least the product trade show was a huge success for the Steele Corporation, so I guess you can't have everything. Now, smile for the camera, Don."

After the photo was taken, Donovan strolled to where his fiancée was standing with his relatives. There was no doubt in Uriel's mind that Donovan would try to work on Natalie again, to move up their wedding date.

Uriel and Ellie had decided not to wait, and figured a Thanksgiving wedding would suit them just fine. They had a lot to be thankful for.

Ellie had accepted a position at Lassiter Industries, and they made Charlotte their primary home, but kept Cavanaugh Lake as their weekend getaway, deciding to keep Uriel's lake house as a guest cottage for any visitors.

The editor at Vandellas Publishing had loved the story and could not believe it had been written by two different people, and had asked Ellie to continue writing as Flame Elbam. Ellie had agreed to do one more book, and she would see how that worked out before doing another.

Uriel smiled as he glanced around the room, looking for his wife, but he didn't see her anywhere. He then scoped all the people who had come to see him and Ellie pledge their love and life to each other. It had been a beautiful affair.

He breathed in deeply when he saw his mother with her boy-toy, but didn't feel so bad when he noted his father was too occupied talking to Donovan's aunt to notice. Or maybe Anthony Lassiter no longer cared, which was even better.

"How much longer for the pics, U?" Xavier leaned over and asked.

"Why are you in such a hurry?" Winston jokingly asked. "It's too early in the day to be making booty calls, X, so chill."

Uriel knew Winston had only been joking, but he had a feeling W's words had hit a nerve with X, and he couldn't help but wonder why. He then glanced over at

Zion. "Thanks for the ring, Z," he said to his godbrother, who had flown in from Rome a couple of days ago.

Zion smiled. "Only for you. I hope she liked it."

Uriel chuckled. "Are you kidding? A wedding set designed by Zion. Come on, man. She loved it."

"I hope you know you're no longer a member of Bachelors in Demand," York decided it was time to point out.

"Whatever," Uriel said, rolling his eyes. He then saw his wife reenter the ballroom with her best friend Darcy. He hadn't forgotten Darcy's role in Ellie's two escapades involving him. He left his godbrothers and moved toward his wife to give her a huge kiss.

When the wedding planner came to grab Ellie for a second, he was left standing with Darcy. "I hear you've moved to New York," he decided to say, while sipping his punch.

She eyed him warily. "Yes, what about it?"

Uriel smiled. "No reason." He knew that, although they were both part of the wedding party, Darcy hadn't officially met York; but Uriel planned for them to meet before he and Ellie left on their honeymoon to Paris. He hid his smile, thinking that an introduction ought to be interesting.

Ellie returned to his side. "The photographer is ready for us to cut the cake."

"All right, but I need to talk to you about something for a minute." He glanced over at Darcy. "Please excuse us for a second."

The moment they stepped out of the ballroom and rounded the corner, he pulled her into his arms and lowered his mouth to hers. She surrendered, and he pulled her closer into his arms and kissed her with a hunger that made her moan.

When he finally withdrew his lips from hers, she pulled in a deep breath. "What was that about?" she asked.

A smile curved his lips and he said, "Inspiration."